GEESE
ARE
NEVER
SWANS

GEESE ARE NEVER SWANS

Created by **KOBE BRYANT**
Written by **EVA CLARK**

GRANITY STUDIOS
COSTA MESA, CALIFORNIA

For S.C.
—*Kobe Bryant*

Part One

Okay, here's what pisses me off: when people don't fucking *listen*. Like right now. I'm standing in this country club driveway and I don't have a car or the gate code. I'm also sweating like crazy—it's got to be at least ninety out—there's an Escalade creeping up my ass, with the driver laying on the horn and everything, like *that's* going to help. I've already explained myself at least three times. But the girl on the other end of this call box still. Won't. Let. Me. In.

Jesus.

The Escalade driver honks again and shouts something. I flip him off. Stupid, but who knows? Maybe he'll be bothered enough to drag his shitty dad-bod down out of his air-conditioned paradise and try to make me *show him some respect* or whatever. I'd kind of like that, to tell you the truth, but I came here for a reason and don't have time for screwing around.

I need to remember that.

"I'm here for Coach Marks!" I shout into the intercom. "The swim coach. He'll want to see me."

"Sir, I already explained. I can't open the gate unless—"

"Tell him I'm Danny Bennett's brother."

"Who?"

I grit my teeth. Ignore the headache simmering in my skull. "Danny. Bennett."

"Hold on." The girl sounds flustered, and it's because she's just realized who I am and why it's important. I figured she would— that's why I said it—but it's also the exact reason I'm here in the first place. I'm sick of being Danny Bennett's brother. I was sick of it before he became a goddamn martyr, and I'm even more sick of it now.

And yeah, sure, it's ironic—my lamenting that without him here I can't do my usual thing of pretending my brother doesn't exist. But these days it's fallen on my shoulders to have to comfort all the people I run into who insist on telling me how sorry they are that he's gone. Supposedly they're sorry for me—that's what they say—but I'm the one who's forced to listen to all their sobby *what could have beens* and *oh God what are we going to do nows*, and it's pretty clear the only person they feel sorry for is themselves.

Bottom line, I hate it. Every second. I wasn't born to be a dead guy's brother, I can tell you that much. My name is Gus Bennett, I'm sixteen years old, and I happen to know for a fact that I'm meant to be someone else. Someone *better*.

So I will be.

2.

Look, I get that there are probably all sorts of ways you're supposed to feel when someone close to you dies. Just like there are probably all sorts of people willing to tell you that however you feel is the right way.

But you should know I'm the kind of person who doesn't want to hear about shit like that. Ever. To my mind, the only thing worse than having to talk about my feelings is listening to someone else pretend to understand them, which is exactly the kind of crap that counselor at my high school tried to pull back in April when I was forced to go see her.

This was also where she confided that the reason we were meeting was that some of my teachers had expressed "concern" over how I was adjusting. Apparently, this concern didn't include coming and talking to me, which says a lot about who they were really concerned for. It's not like my silence meant I was planning on shooting up the school or anything. Kind of the opposite, although according to the counselor, the one thing you're *definitely* supposed to do when your older brother comes home from college to hang himself is blab to a stranger about it.

"It's okay to feel angry. Or guilty," she told me in that well-trained-therapist voice of hers, the one that's meant to go down easy and get you to puke up a bunch of tears or confessions or life-affirming moments of brilliance and insight. "It's all part of the grieving process."

"I'm not angry," I told her, pushing my chair back, getting ready to leave. Plato once said the measure of a man is what he does with his power, but I believe the inverse to be true. What matters is what he does with *anything*. At any time. Isn't that where power comes from? "And I don't feel guilty, either. You know what I feel right now? Good. Better than good. Because I'm fucking free."

And then finally, there it is—the best damn feeling on earth. Well, barring sex, I've been told, but I'll have to get back to you on that when I actually . . . know. That's not likely to be anytime soon, however, and there ought to be a word for the paradox of wanting so badly to be with another person while at the same time needing to be completely alone. Regardless, this moment is sweet. This moment is what I live for.

Victory.

The club's six-foot-high wrought-iron access gates swing open, granting me entrance. The girl from the call box doesn't say anything and she doesn't have to; we both know I've won. Never the type for false modesty—or any other kind—I square my shoulders and hold my head high as I walk onto the property, marching straight beneath carved lettering that reads *Lafayette Country Club ~ Members Only.*

For better or for worse, I have arrived.

But because life is shit, and other people even shittier, that idiot SUV follows right on my heels. My instinct is to walk slowly— the universal passive-aggressive symbol for *fuck you*—forcing Mr. Escalade to either run me over or allow me to be the object of his petty ire for a few minutes more. But it's not worth it. Not today. There are ways to win by cutting your losses, and to this end, I veer off the main road and hoof it down the dirt trail leading to the aquatic center.

The clubhouse, tennis courts, and main parking lot are all

situated on the opposite end of the grounds, so my walk to the pool is a solitary one. Sweaty, too. A June morning in California means sprinklers on the golf course, our five-year drought be damned, but the sun is unforgiving. A fellow grudge holder, I admire this in a way, but it's not like I don't know the UV rays are killing me. It's not like I can't admire that, too.

Mt. Diablo and a handful of other craggy peaks hover in the distance, rising tall against the cloudless sky. In contrast to the club's eighteen-hole emerald lushness, the grass and brush on those faraway hills have all turned yellow, which is another word for dead. And while it doesn't surprise me that rich people believe they're owed more than what nature's willing to give, I still think it really fucking sucks.

Christ. This whole thing's taking too long. Hopping over a smiley face–adorned *Please Stay on the Path!* sign so cheerful I could barf, I abandon the trail and cut across the green, taking care to trample a few flowers in the process. My shoes are wet in seconds, petals smashed and stuck everywhere, but that's the least of my concerns. I need to focus on the task ahead. I need to get what I came for. Like my brother used to say: practice is where intent is born. And for all his failings, he definitely got that one right. So in my mind, I go over the things I want to say.

The way I want to say them.

Don't be a dick, the good part of my brain warns.

Be polite.

Be humble.

I keep walking, my shoes keep tearing up turf, and before the swim complex even comes into view, I can hear pool noises—the wild clamor of voices, the shrill blast of a whistle, the near-constant *smack-splash* of humans leaping from land into the depths of a watery underworld.

These are sounds I know well. Too well, you could say, and it's almost as if they're a part of me, living in my bones, writhing up my spine, able to kick-start a force within me so primal that reality as

I know it pales. For a shimmering instant, I can actually *smell* the pool—the sharp sting-scent of chlorine fumes and zinc oxide, the must of wet clothes, the reek of stale rubber, and the sticky sweetness of melted Otter Pops—although I know that's impossible. But this is how memory works, I guess: honesty rubbed raw by anticipation, by what *matters*, and while it's clear that every cell in my body lies primed and gut-loaded with the past, I also believe that the truth lies in the present.

It *has* to.

And yeah, in case you haven't figured it out by now, I'm a swimmer, too. No, I'm not the one you've heard of, but that's not due to lack of talent—only access. In fact, I've spent the last two years on my high school's team, swimming my ass off and setting school records. Our medley team even went to state last month on account of my performance. Well, *I* didn't get to go, actually, because of all the shit that went down, but I should've been there. It could've been my moment. My breakout. My time to prove my brother wrong, once and for all.

But I wasn't able to be there. Thanks to him.

So now, motherfucker, I'm here.

4.

Skimming along the far edge of the golf course, I make my way through the trees, the shade, the fiddlehead ferns. Dust and pine needles cling to my wet shoes, and as I come around a sharp bend, that's when I see it—the LCC aquatic center, in all its pristine and sprawling glory.

There's the red tile roof and stucco walls.

The bobbing lane lines.

The blue, blue depths.

Nothing about this place has changed, and it makes me sick. Every goddamn inch of it.

There's a saying among swimmers that each pool's the same so long as it's filled with water. But I don't know. There's something different about this one. It's the history, I guess. The club itself is a place where the ultra-rich can waste the finite hours of their lives alongside tennis pros and caddies rather than their families. But admittance to the elite LCC swim team—and its peerless reputation—is based on merit. Okay, it's based on money, too. I'd be a fool to suggest otherwise. But it's the place where talent meets means. And it's where it all happened for Danny. The good stuff, at least.

The rest came later.

My sickness intensifies, edging up my throat as I slip through the spring-close gate and step into organized chaos. I'm able to swallow it down, but being here is Dante's-ninth-circle-of-hell bad. It's peak training time—kids are everywhere, shrieking, flailing, in the water, on the deck—and I know where I'm going and what it is I need to do, but I kind of can't take it. Which is pathetic. I brought myself here, didn't I? But logic eludes my nerves as I squeeze past the diving team training off a row of springboards set in increasing height, and I do what I have to in order to keep my shit together.

I stop to watch.

Naturally, their pool is the deepest, stretching twelve feet beneath the earth. That's far enough to make your ears pop, or 5.2 pounds per square inch, if you want to get technical. Not exactly an insignificant amount of pressure, although no one's climbing the platform tower today, a full twenty-five feet from the ground. They're just working the three- and six-meter boards, and even so, it's a thrill to see their acrobatic feats of daring, those fatalistic twists and turns. Only it's not long before the spinning hurts my head, a queasy-making ache born from my more rigid nature. This makes sense, if you think about it—divers embrace gravity, the fact that our bodies are made to sink. Us swimmers, on the other hand, work by way of avoidance; we're doing all we can to forget it.

I once tried explaining this to Danny, on some rare occasion when I got the urge to bond with him over this thing we both did. He was lifting weights in the garage while I watched, and I told him I thought swimming was a sport of delusion. That madness was what fueled greatness and that *that* was the fire we walked by delving beneath the surface and daring to come back up again.

But he just laughed in response—in truth, he hardly considered what I did actual swimming, as if we weren't both doing our best not to drown—and told me that wasn't the way he saw it. Not in the least.

"Then how do you see it?" I stared up at him from where I sat on the cold cement floor, foolishly wide-eyed and eager for his answer. I was still a dumb kid then. I still believed he was something more.

My brother didn't pause in his set. The weights were huge— those plates weighed more than I did—but he kept curling his biceps while sweat poured from his body, dripped onto my shoe. "You know how they call horse racing the sport of kings?"

I shook my head. I didn't know.

"Well, they do," he said between gasps. "But swimming, it's something even better."

"What's that?" I asked.

Contract and release. Danny grunted, squeezed his eyes shut tight as he grimaced through the pain. "It's the sport of *gods*."

5

Well, if gods are man-made, then this is the place of creation. The divers break, and I edge past the huge glass-boxed display chronicling the club's forty-year history of aquatic bragging rights. It's tacky, but they've earned those rights, launching no less than nine Olympic medalists, six of whom brought home gold. My brother was supposed to be the tenth, the seventh, and the best, of course, and maybe it's just me, but I'm picking up an air of rebellion from this collection of accolades: the bold showcasing of flag after flag, banner after banner, and trophy after trophy. A whole glittering trove of glory. Danny didn't make it, but our excellence is not in doubt, it all says.

How could it be?

Well, for my part, I'm neither intimidated nor impressed. I don't need trophies to know what they've done. I just need them to keep doing it so I can reap a little of that glory for myself.

Arriving at the far end of the lap pool, I close in on the blocks where the swim team is training. This late in the morning, swim lessons are winding down; all that remains is a group of ten- or eleven-year-old girls who are practicing their starts. For good reason: the dive from the blocks is one of the best predictors of overall performance, and it's clear their parents know this. Keeping watch from the bleachers, they're huddled like birds on a wire, with their hands clasped tight, their eyes wide, every one of them searching desperately for a sign, any sign, that their kid is special. Distinctive, in some way.

They aren't, from what I can tell, and that's not me being a total asshole. I'm sure these girls are some of the best swimmers in their age-group. I'm sure they have walls of ribbons and years of lessons behind them, and they've been told they have what it takes. But I see the way they keep glancing at their parents, and I know whose dream it is they're here to fulfill. Trust me, Danny never looked at our mom that way when she was up in those bleachers. He never looked at anyone, except the one person he trusted to help make his dream a reality.

This also happens to be the person I'm here to see. I stopped watching Danny do anything years ago, but it's only been six weeks since I last ran into Coach Marks. That was at the funeral, and for an elite coach renowned as he is for his alleged stoicism and strength, he was a lot weepier than I expected. Or personally cared to witness. He ended up staying in the church after everyone else left, with his head down, a Bible in his lap, and he was just sobbing. I don't even think my mom cried that much and she's a fucking fountain these days.

He pulled it together somehow, though, because he showed up at the wake hours later. Even then, his eyes were red and puffy, his dove-gray suit all wrinkled, and he didn't let up on the bourbon the whole time he was in our house. To be fair, I didn't either, and there were a couple times that afternoon where I got the feeling he wanted to talk to me. But a lot of people did that day, and you know, I'm not dumb. With the exception of a couple of classmates who dropped by to offer their condolences, the person everyone wanted to talk to wasn't *me*. They all wanted a piece of Danny, however small or fleeting or flat-out wrong, and figured I'd just feel lucky for the chance to step into that role.

I bailed on that shitshow as soon as I could. I'm not totally unsympathetic to other people's pain, but I needed time alone with my own. That night, when I left, I took the bourbon with me, riding my bike down to the reservoir and crawling onto the rocks by the shore, not far from the pier. I stayed there until well after dark, listening to the water lap against the pilings, while getting piss-drunk on Knob Creek and wishing my brother had never been born so no one would feel compelled to make such a fucking tragedy out of his death.

But still, there was something about seeing Coach Marks that day that got me thinking. About *my* life. My future.

About what it is I need to do and how he'll help me get there.

6.

"Hey, Coach," I say as I approach.

Remember the don't-be-a-dick thing, I warn myself.

Be polite. Be respectful.

But get what you came for.

He's standing poolside in full sun, LCC visor shading his face, clipboard in hand, watching his girls and demanding perfection, and *this* is the Coach Marks I remember—tall, weathered skin, gray hair, impossible to read but with squinting eyes that see *everything*. And I guess I assumed the call-box girl would've told him I was coming after she let me in because that seems like the normal, decent human thing to do. But what do I know about decent? Not a lot, it turns out, because it's clear by the way Coach Marks looks up at me that the girl didn't tell him shit.

"Danny," he says.

"Gus," I reply.

He falters, his chill-as-fuck mask slipping momentarily as he realizes his mistake, and if I were the kind of guy who knew how to feel guilty for the things I did or the ways I hurt people, I'd probably feel that way now.

But I don't.

Coach Marks stammers. "Right! Gus. Of course. I'm sorry. It's just, you look like him. I thought . . ."

"I need to talk to you," I say.

"Now?"

"Yeah. I mean, if that's cool?"

He nods, still visibly flustered. Turns and yells something to his swimmers, then gestures for me to follow him away from the water into the shade of the pool house. Here he sets his clipboard down, blows air through his cheeks, then offers me his full attention, something those bleacher parents would no doubt kill for. "It's good to see you, Gus."

"Thanks. You too."

"How's your mom doing?"

"Not great."

"I'm sorry to hear that."

I shrug. Look away.

"At the funeral," Coach Marks says. "We didn't get a chance to talk, you and I."

"I know."

"Well, I wanted to tell you that I understand a little of what you're going through. Losing a brother, no matter when it happens, it's . . . it's not easy."

"I really don't want to talk about the funeral," I say quickly. "That's not why I'm here."

Coach Marks frowns. "It's not?"

"No. And hey, look, it wasn't your fault what happened to Danny. It had nothing to do with you. Seriously. Okay?"

This last bit I genuinely intend as kindness, words offered as balm, but I've miscalculated somehow. The coach's jaw tightens. He lifts his chin. "What's up, then? How can I help you?"

"I want to swim for you," I say.

"What?"

"I'm good enough. Hell, I'm better than good. I've been swimming at Acalanes High for the past two years. All-state for both. Multiple school records. You can check out my times. Figure if I come here, I can get on the national circuit for you in the fall. Then I'll make the national team, qualify for the Olympics. Swim for the US in Tokyo next year. Just like, you know, he wanted to."

Coach Marks says nothing. He just stares at me.

Give it to me, I think. *Come on. Please. Just give me this one goddamn thing.*

I brace myself, prepared to argue my worth. But what he finally says is: "Why?"

My nose wrinkles. "Why what?"

"Why do you want to swim for *me*?"

What kind of question is that? "Same reason as everybody. You're the best. You almost got Danny to the top."

"But I didn't."

"But I'll get there. I know I will."

"So you think you're better than Danny?"

"I will be."

Skepticism lines the coach's face, a shadowed ridging of doubt. "Acalanes, you say?"

"Yup. I swim free. Got school records in both the two hundred and the five. Plus the individual medley and the relay. But I mean, I can swim anything you need me to."

"Uh-huh. And how old are you, Gus?"

"Sixteen. Almost seventeen."

"Danny came to me when he was twelve."

"Okay."

"Well, if you're so good, why'd you wait five years?"

Why indeed? I roll my shoulders. Meet his gaze. "There's only room for one champion in a household."

Coach Marks is incredulous. "Is that really what you believe?"

"*No.*" I snort. "But it's what Danny told me."

My brother used to say there were three things that separated good athletes from the great ones. But Danny being Danny, he never told me what they were.

The first isn't hard to figure out. It had to be something like *Never stop to help anyone who's drowning; otherwise no one will ever bother learning to swim*. Or maybe it was *Survival of the fittest; because they've fucking earned it*. Pragmatic, I suppose, but also cruel—which is a pretty apt description of Danny's philosophy toward just about anything. What the other two were is anyone's guess. Although given the recent choice he made in the face of failure, it's safe to say he got at least one of them wrong.

Personally, I've got my own ideas of what does and doesn't make greatness, and seeing as I'm still around to prove my point, I've got no problem sharing what they are. Maybe that makes me a hypocrite or whatever because I value autonomy more than listening to the bullshit other people come up with, but the most important thing I've learned in my sixteen years on earth is this: don't ever let anyone tell you what you *can't* do.

And yeah, I know that sounds like some dippy inspirational message, the kind you're supposed to tape to your bathroom mirror and read out loud every morning so you don't forget that your shitty life circumstances are all your own fucking fault. But see, that's the thing about *personal responsibility*; it's sold as empowerment, a means of transcendence or the true path to righteousness. But from what I can tell, what people really mean when they use that phrase has a lot less to do with taking ownership of their own lives than it does with justifying why they're not bothering to care about anyone else's.

Anyway, that's not the kind of shit I'm talking about. I'm just done letting other people tell me what they think is best for me. Or worse, that I shouldn't want the things I need. That's something I've thought about a lot over the past six weeks. How people only tell you your dreams are impossible when they're scared you might reach them.

So it's a vote of confidence, really.

Danny was a good example of this. He was barely thirteen when he qualified for his first junior national event. It was held out in Philadelphia and they ended up televising it, on account of his age. And the thing is, Danny had earned his spot. He'd fought for it, and against all biological and predictive odds, he won. Yet every single person he met that weekend—coaches, older swimmers, parents, even league reps—worked hard to put him in his place. One by one, they made a point of coming over and telling him the same damn thing: that he was *lucky* to be there. You know, for the experience.

Well, most people in the swimming world can remember what happened next—how my brother didn't give a shit about luck. How he got in that pool and smoked his events. Ended up ranked in the top twenty by the end of the year and was on university recruitment lists before he'd even finished middle school. He was set for life, at that point. Glory bound. Destined for gold and the record books. Destined to be a legend.

He never looked back after that.

Until, you know, he did.

8.

I stand up tall, stick out my chest, and this, *this* is the moment I came for. A moment of wrong-righting and redemption. Of reckoning, even. Because like the fault lines running beneath this shaky California town, putting us at the whim of friction and fate, the aftermath of my family's own tectonic crumbling has fundamentally redrawn our boundaries.

And not always for the worse.

So I smile broadly at Coach Marks as he appraises me, as he soaks me in. I don't mind being judged when I know where I stand; I can back up every claim I've made. And in terms of sheer genetic potential, I'm practically the gift horse he's already owned and lost.

There's only one answer he can give, clearly, which is why I don't understand when I hear him utter the words "I'm sorry."

"Wait, what?" I ask.

Coach Marks bends for his clipboard, strokes his chin, and looks back at the girls. The attention I commanded is dissolving into a froth of nothingness. "I'm sorry," he says again, and the worst part is that his tone is sincere. He means what he says. "I'm not looking for another swimmer right now, Gus. I'm just not. But best of luck to you."

I'm speechless. My cheeks blaze, and I mean, this is some serious bullshit. Who the *fuck* does he think he is? There's nothing I want to do more than grab that stupid whistle and wring his neck with the goddamn cord. But as he turns to walk away—to *dismiss* me—that's when he really does it. Coach Marks has the nerve to reach out with one hand and actually *squeeze my shoulder*. Like he's my dad or something. Like he wants me to believe he gives a damn about my feelings.

Flesh to flame. I jerk my shoulder back with a snarl. Coach Marks looks up at me and I know what he sees in my eyes. And I know he knows he's wrong about this. Rejecting me out of some misguided loyalty to the swimmer who rejected *him* only perpetuates the same fucked-up shit that got us here in the first place. Not to mention, it's also bad judgment. He's the one who lost Danny. The ultimate rejection: my brother ditched him for his college coach a year before he died. So the issue isn't whether Coach Marks is the answer to all *my* problems—it's that we both know I could be the answer to his.

Screw it. Whatever the fuck that was, it's over. Coach Marks tries saying something else, some words of condolence or empty blathering meant to excuse his shitty choices and piss-poor reasoning. Well, he's an idiot if he thinks I have any intention of sticking around to hear what he has to say.

I turn on my heel and go. A rash of pettiness runs through me, and as I pass the shallow end of the pool, I dig deep, scraping the bottom of my lungs and spitting straight into the water. A group of masters swimmers glare at me through their goggles, but I must appear adequately murderous because no one says a word.

Then I'm out of there. Kick-slamming my way through the pool gate, I march toward the club entrance, that gate I had to use my brother's name to get through. My long legs carry me over the grounds quickly, away from this hellish cesspool, and as I make my escape, I tell myself all the things I need to hear:

That Coach Marks is a flaccid dick.

That I'll find another, better way without him.

That he's going to regret what he's done, I'll make damn sure of that.

And see, this is the dark truth about coaching. The part that really pisses me off because it's the part us swimmers aren't meant to know: this whole enterprise is built on smoke and mirrors. It's less delusion than illusion, perhaps, but coaching's a field founded on superstition and rumor far more than skill and methodology.

Like the Bible, swimming has its own lore, its stories and reverence and articles of faith that have been handed down, year after year, team after team, and lap after lap. The impact of this is as telling as the tides, witnessed in the swift, seasonal murmuration of glory-eyed swimmers, all breaking to chase the same fad, the same coach, the same legend, the same answer. Whatever it is they've been told they need in order to make it where others have gone.

What they don't know, however, is that you can't win by following in someone else's wake. By definition, you've already lost. My wanting to train with Coach Marks has nothing to do with chasing what worked for Danny. It's about sparking the glorious blaze of energy our pairing would inspire. Seeing me, the younger brother, rising from the flames of tragedy in order to join with Danny's grieving and guilt-ridden coach is pure myth in the making.

It's a story that would have every crowd on their feet, cheering for my victory, and that's the shit that matters. I'm talking on a spiritual level. Last year I watched *When We Were Kings*, the film about Foreman and Ali and the Rumble in the Jungle, and you can actually see that force in action. It was everything sport can be. Not just winning a boxing match or even mastery of physical prowess. It was about *more*, about Muhammad Ali leaving nothing to chance. He flew to Zaire and he gave the people who came to watch everything, every piece of himself. They absorbed his passion until they wanted to be a part of his story. So it was transcendent, heroic, even, the way these gifts came back to him tenfold when he needed them.

The way that crowd carried him home.

The thing is, no matter who *I* train with, I'll have some of that mythology with me just by the nature of who I am and where I come from. The shadow of my brother's death will make people want to love me, want to light the fire that guides my flame.

I'll let them, of course. I have no qualms about exploiting Danny's legacy, and I plan on doing it with or without Coach Marks. But he could've come with me. It would've been special—that's why I was willing to offer him a piece of my gilded destiny in the first place. But his rejection is proof positive that beneath that stoicism and mystery, there's nothing to him at all, just a sad old man standing behind a curtain who doesn't even know when to pull the right strings anymore.

That's the *other* dirty secret of coaching. The one they better hope like hell our superstition and delusion will drown out and wash away. Because the truth is, they're all cowards. More status quo than revolutionary. More false patriot than rebel. They don't seek out what they don't know—like the kid who's circumvented private lessons and country club training to come up on his own by swimming for his public high school—because they don't want anything about this system to change. Sameness is their lifeblood. Their living. Which means Coach Marks not taking me on isn't because he's afraid he'll fail.

He's afraid he won't.

10.

"Gus! Hey, Gus!"

I'm nearing the top of the hill when I hear someone call my name. It's a distant voice and I spin around, confused, only to see a group of well-dressed people lingering outside on the flagstone patio of one of the club's ivy-covered outbuildings. I squint but can't figure out what's going on. It looks they're having a business meeting. Or a baby christening. Or who the hell knows? I mean, it's Wednesday morning and these people are wearing pastels and sport coats and drinking what looks like champagne out of fluted glasses. Whatever it is that's going on, it's safe to say I don't know anyone who'd be at an event like this. So I turn back around.

Keep walking.

"Gus!" The voice goes up an octave and it's more urgent now. Less warm. Maybe that Escalade driver found out who I am and put a bounty on my head. But when I turn to look again, that's when I see her. It's a *girl*—Ashley Browning, to be precise—and she's walking in my direction. Ashley goes to my school and we're in the same grade, so we know each other, obviously, but it's not like we're friends. At all.

So why is she coming toward me?

Well, despite appearances to the contrary, I do have some fucking manners, so I stop, shove my hands in my pockets, and try my best not to look pissed off. She draws closer and I guess whatever's happening on the patio isn't a business event, since trust me, Ashley Browning doesn't need a summer job and even if she did, she still wouldn't get one, which probably tells you something about the Brownings. They're not only the type who would've liked it when the band kept playing after the *Titanic* hit that iceberg; they would've complained to the management if they hadn't. Anyway, at the moment, Ashley's got on this shiny turquoise dress and heels that are absolutely not made for wet grass. They keep sinking and she ends up having to hop her way over to me.

She actually laughs while she does this, which gets me to relax a little. As a rule I don't like people talking to me, but as a rule, people usually don't. This mostly goes double for girls, with some rare exceptions.

"Hey," she says when she reaches me. "I didn't know you were coming. My mom didn't mention it."

"Mention what?" I ask, and I can't help but stare at her bare shoulders, at the line of sweat beading along her clavicle.

Ashley doesn't bother answering. Instead she grabs my hand and pulls me with her, dragging me back across the lawn in the direction she just came from.

For a few steps, I let her do this. The air's ripe with eucalyptus oil, the scent of gardenias, and no, I don't like Ashley, but there's something in her touch, that vital press of skin on skin. It's alluring, undeniably so, and while my brain may not, the rest of me wants it, these feelings that are bubbling to the surface—the breathless wash of heat, that bright rush of desire, all followed by a dizzying flood of memories, not of the girl who's currently touching me, but of *her*.

I stop walking.

"Ashley," I say as she turns to look at me, her brown eyes wide and her glossed lips pursed tight in an obvious expression of *what the fuck are you doing?*

"I need to go," I tell her.

"What?"

I pull my hand free. "I can't be here."

"Then why'd you come?"

"I *didn't*." I gesture at the patio. "I don't even know what this is."

"My parents' anniversary brunch."

"Oh."

"They said they wanted to see you. It'd mean a lot to them." She looks over her shoulder, her hair swaying in a unified grace that mystifies me. "Plus Lainey's coming later."

Now I feel weak. Ashley's sister Lainey is different than the rest of the Brownings, and for as close as we were at one point in time, I've always wished we were closer. I've always wished for what I couldn't have. "She is?"

Ashley nods. "She keeps saying she's going to call you about the scholarship. I know she wants you involved."

"What scholarship?"

"The one my parents are setting up in Danny's name. You don't know about it?"

"No."

"It's for here at the club. Ten grand a year to a young swimmer with promise. They're going to announce later in the summer, I guess, at some big event. Pretty sure your mom knows the details."

I'm confused. "But you aren't swimmers. Why would your family do that?"

"What do you mean why?" Ashley shoots another look over her shoulder. Like she's hoping someone will come and rescue her. "Because they care about Danny?"

"Well, they shouldn't bother," I say. "It'll be a total fucking waste."

"You could be a little more grateful about it. My family's done a lot for yours over the years."

"Oh yeah? And what, exactly, have they done for *me*?"

Ashley's lip curls. "They don't need to do anything!"

"Then neither do I," I growl, and while this conversation's clearly over, I'm not willing to be the one to walk away. Not this time. So I stand there in the grass, with my arms folded and my eyes narrowed, until Ashley Browning seethes with fury and calls me a self-entitled bitch. She uses the word *crazy*, too, which is rich seeing as I'm not the one who wants to hand out money to a kid in honor of a guy who wrapped a belt around his neck until his eyes bled.

I don't argue any of this with her, a fact that only makes her more furious. Eventually she leaves, flouncing back to her family, where she'll no doubt tell them how terrible an excuse for a human I am, an utter disgrace to the memory of my perfect dead brother who's hurt them far more than I ever could. It's pathetic, really, everything about the Brownings, the things they love and choose to be, and while thoughts of her sister pierce the surface of my mind, skimming along deep-worn grooves of longing and despair, I watch Ashley abandon me with only one thought running through my mind.

Good.

11.

I'm alone again. Everything feels different. Worse, really, which is hard to explain, seeing as aloneness usually ranks up there with winning and the sex I've never had as shit I'd sacrifice just about anything for. Even harder to explain is the fact that while I should want nothing more than to spread my wings and bust ass out of this place, I don't.

Instead I turn and head right back down the perfectly manicured hillside toward the aquatic center. It's like walking the plank or stepping up to the gallows—there's a sense of destiny in doing what's unlikely to end well. Only this time, I don't enter the actual pool area. I walk farther, making my way toward the staff parking lot, which is at the far end of the property, hidden from public view by a tall corral of redwood fencing.

I clench my hands into fists and open them again. It's near midday and the sun's high in the sky, no longer fucking around with shadows or mountains to hide its glare. But even beneath this washed-out spotlight heat, something dark writhes within these country club walls. I can feel it, here, in this place, but also inside me, having been stirred up, agitated and exposed, by what Ashley told me about the scholarship her family's putting together.

The one in Danny's name.

Just thinking about it is enough to make me claw my throat, rub my aching chest. What gets me is knowing I'll never hear the end of it. Once this scholarship takes off, gets in the press—and it will—it'll be Danny, Danny, Danny. Danny the hero, for-fucking-ever. Even more than it already is.

This is the reason I'm still here, still wallowing around in this place I've always hated and which has never welcomed me. You see, for a long time, I was like everyone else. Brainwashed into believing the best thing I could do was sit in the stands and cheer for my brother's success. Over and over, I watched him dive into that pool to race the black stripe running along the bottom. He always won—every goddamn time—but you know what? All those years and all those pools, and not once did anyone ever ask why I wasn't in the water. No one cared if I had dreams of my own because caring about me meant taking something away from Danny.

But loneliness has its merit. Resentment, too. Eventually I figured out the only thing worth worrying about was myself, and so selfishness became my act of rebellion. An act of survival. It still is, really, which is why I plan on making this stupid thing with Coach Marks work.

Survival isn't enough anymore. I have other needs and darker dreams. These days my lot in life is making sure my asshole of a brother stays dead. I don't care how that sounds. He hasn't earned the right to immortality, and I sure as hell won't let anyone give it to him. Of all the things in my life I don't think I could live with, *that's* at the top of my goddamn list.

12.

I bide my time lurking between a silver Lexus coupe with a faded *USA Swimming* sticker on the bumper and a bright green Vanagon that's got Bernie shit plastered all over it, along with a handmade sign proclaiming *JESUS WAS A SOCIALIST*. Sunlight ricochets off metal to roast my skin until I swear I can smell it—like a pig on a spit—and you know, truth be told, I'm kind of curious who this Vanagon belongs to because my guess is they won't last long around here.

This is my logic talking, by the way, not my politics. By definition, the LCC's no place for socialism, not even the watered-down European kind. It's basically capitalism personified and no one who pays twenty grand a year to walk their red-blooded ass around these eighteen holes wants to be reminded that their privilege depends on the subjugation of others. Personally, I don't think it's anywhere close to subversive to have a sign on your car highlighting the wealth-distributing virtues of Jesus, but around here, it kind of is.

Quick check of my phone. I've been in the staff parking lot for more than two hours, which is seriously starting to suck. The phone's battery's hovering in the red, but there's no point saving it for later. I plunk my ass in the gravel and drain what's left by way of watching old clips of world record swims. My favorite, far and away, is Thorpe's 400 m freestyle at the Sydney Games. In part because it's close to my best distance. But he also had such *composure*. He never did that American thing of screaming and making a fucking scene when he won, as if people would have no idea he was happy if he didn't tell them in the most obnoxious way possible. Nah, he just let his time on the clock do the talking. There's a lot to be said for keeping shit to yourself.

Right then, a crunch of gravel gets me to lift my head, and when I look up, it's *him*. Coach Marks. He's crossing the parking lot and I scramble to my feet, brushing dust from my legs, my hands, and popping up from behind the Lexus so fast I must look like a stalker. My phone tumbles to the ground but I don't reach for it.

"Coach." I force cheer and lightness I don't feel into my voice. *I am not a threatening person*, this voice says. *I'm not lying in wait or trying to scare you. I'm simply here to have a Reasonable Conversation that I hope will encourage you to reconsider your earlier decision.*

Or else.

Coach Marks frowns at the sight of me. No more mistaking me for my brother—he knows who I am this time. "What is it, Gus? You been waiting out here for me all day?"

I nod. My head buzzes from getting up so fast and colored lights dot my visual field, but I grit my teeth and hold on to consciousness by an act of sheer will.

"Why?" he asks.

"Because I can do it," I say in a rush. "I can win for you. I can win it all. Everything Danny couldn't."

"You said that already."

"Well, I mean it."

"So you actually believe you're going to make the Olympics next year? At your age? With your experience? Or lack of it. Do you know how that sounds?" A taunting edge colors his tone.

"Thorpe did it at sixteen," I retort.

He waves a hand. "And Phelps was even younger when he qualified. Yeah, I know. But that's not the point."

"Phelps didn't do shit that year," I mutter.

"What was that?"

"Thorpe's the one who won gold in his first Games. Not Phelps."

Coach Marks gives me a funny look, almost an appraising one, but there's something else lingering in his eyes, in the way he sees me. It's something I don't like.

Pity.

"Look," he says. "I'd love to give you a shot. I really would. Any brother of Danny's . . . well, you're someone I'd like to get to know. On your terms. But there'll be time for that later. I promise. You don't need to be worrying about training at the highest level while you're going through a loss like this. It's a lot to ask of anyone, at any time. But right now, you need to grieve. You need to be with your mom. What your family's going through, it's hard, you know?"

My head feels like it might burst. Right here. All over everything.

"Fuck you," I snarl.

He blinks. "What?"

"You don't know what I need. You don't know anything about me!"

Coach Marks takes a step back. "Is this how you talk to your coach at Acalanes?"

Shit. I rub my chest. Try to calm myself down. "*No*. Look, I'm sorry I said that. I'm just . . . I'm *pissed*. You don't want me, say you don't want me. But don't try and sell me some bullshit about how what you're doing is for my benefit. Because what I *need* is to do what Danny couldn't. And I plan on doing it with or without you."

Coach Marks pauses. "Okay."

"Okay what?"

"Okay." He holds up his hands. "You're right. I'm sorry. It's not my place to tell you how to grieve. You need to do what's right for you. Absolutely."

"You mean that?"

"Sure. Everyone grieves differently. If swimming's what helps, that's what you should be doing. No judgment."

"So I can swim for you?"

"I didn't say that. But . . ."

"But what?" I press.

He softens. "We've got practice tomorrow at five thirty a.m.

You show up, work out with my team. I'll take a look. All right? Tell you what I think."

"And if I'm good enough?"

"Then we'll talk."

"I'll be there."

"Good," he says. "And, Gus?"

"Huh?"

"Just so I understand where you're coming from. Are you saying you want to finish Danny's dream of being in the Olympics as a way of honoring him?"

My spine stiffens. "Not exactly."

"Then why does doing it now matter so much?"

"It matters because I'm my own swimmer. I don't want to be compared to Danny anymore."

"You don't?"

"No," I say. "I want *him* to be compared to *me*."

13.

Coach Marks throws his head back and laughs, like what I just said was a joke or a show of Danny-esque bravado. I'm not joking, but I know better than to say that. I also know better than to stick around and let my mouth ruin a good thing. So after thanking Coach Marks for his time, I reach for my dropped phone, reiterate my vow to show up in the morning—a statement he appears to take more as a threat than a promise—and leave.

Once again, I head back up the hill toward the main gate, and it's weird. I got what I wanted, yet I can't shake the feeling I'm a shitty person for asking for it in the first place. It's not that I wasn't honest about my intentions—I was—but Coach Marks looked so damn sad talking about Danny. Haunted, even, and the thing is, I know he feels bad about what happened and wishes there were something he could've done. I just really wish that he didn't.

My bike's right where I stashed it: deep in the woods that run adjacent to the club, not locked but well hidden behind a scrubby patch of pink and purple oleander and a clump of what looks suspiciously like poison oak—tight clusters of branches adorned with oily leaves of three. Technically, this place is public land, part of the East Bay Regional Park system, which is the reason I felt safe leaving my bike here and not closer to the club. Even without a Bernie sticker or other signs of socialist inclinations, the groundskeepers there would've tossed this piece of shit in a dumpster based on looks alone.

Swinging my leg over the rusty crossbar, I start the long ride home as afternoon traffic picks up. Commuters speed down this road to avoid the highway, and there are enough white bicycle memorials along my route to ensure that I harbor no illusions about my mortality. I wouldn't anyway. Car crashes are my kryptonite and my mind is relentless in the way it flips through images of endless bike-versus-car scenarios and the subsequent bloody outcomes. This doesn't mean the urge isn't there to flip off every Volvo that veers too close or takes a turn too wide. But unlike my interaction with the Escalade this morning, confrontation on the open road won't get me anywhere but dead.

I opt for personal masochism instead, hitting the hills hard and taking them at a punishing speed that can only be maintained by standing up, shifting gears, and sprinting like an ox until my quads burn and my guts jam up somewhere beneath my ribs. It's worth it for the downhill, though, the glide and bliss of pure flight. The wind slaps my face, milks tears from my eyes, but I can take it, the pain, the discomfort. I can take it all.

And then I'll take more.

14.

Role reversal: I coast into downtown Lafayette, where pedestrians flood the streets with little to no self-awareness. I spy small children darting every which way; old people taking multiple light cycles to move from curb to curb; and dumbasses who don't bother looking in any direction—much less both—before stepping into the street with earbuds in and their phones out. And while I don't personally want the responsibility of keeping any of these folks alive, I also don't want to be the one to kill them. So I slow down.

Use the appropriate amount of caution.

This town is what the soulless call quaint, although even I can admit that summer's when it's got the most shine. With its wide sidewalks, bougie storefronts, and shady oak trees, this place is essentially an extension of the country club, offering the sweet promise of endless days and the indulgence of all of California's bounty. It's a promise for the wealthy, of course, but it's also a lie. There's no romance buried here or even aspiration, just the eternal mindlessness of the masses, eager to play out the role they've been given, to smile and nod and warm their hands on this shitshow of a world that's burning down around us.

It feels different to be riding my bike down Main Street, knowing Danny's gone, although it's hard to put a finger on why. It's not like we ever rode together . . . or did anything else together. Not if he could help it. But despite the impact he had in the pool, I doubt any of these people knew him on a personal level. It's possible they showed up at one of the endless tributes held in his honor. Maybe they even lit a candle. Shed a tear. Said a prayer. Or maybe they simply heard how he died and lamented to whoever would listen at the time about the pressures of youth sports these days while simultaneously shelling out five figures for their kid's soccer club dues.

Turning off Main past the local Peet's Coffee, I weave through a curling network of tree-lined roads and drought-tolerant landscaping, which is more virtue signaling than virtue. Soon the houses begin to spread out. They grow smaller and less stately, and sit farther back from the street, giving the neighborhood a more rural feel. I cut a right on Lynnwood Court and coast the last bit toward home.

My mother's car is parked in the driveway, coated in summer dust like a weary ghost. Her car's always here these days because she can't go places without losing her mind. At first I thought it was because she was afraid she'd be reminded of Danny—that she'd run into some small piece of him that would reopen her wounds in a public bloodletting. But the truth is she'd rather wallow, stagnant in her endless sorrow, than risk creating a memory he'll never be a part of.

Our house sits at the very end of the court. Once noble, it's now a teetering Spanish Colonial with an overgrown yard and a rotting roof that backs up to a burbling stream and a steep hillside dotted with oak trees and grazing cattle. This area is quiet and suburban and supposedly safe. It was nice once, too, which isn't to say it's not now, but there are newer, better neighborhoods nearby and ones with more prestige. This also happens to be the home my mother grew up in; she inherited it from her parents. That's meant to be nice, too—parents providing for their children, even in death. But if you ask me, there's a fine line between gift and obligation, and I have yet to figure out whether *nice* is truly a blessing or a curse.

The front gate latch sticks and I have to put my shoulder into it to force my way in. After kicking the rickety thing shut behind me, I drop my bike in the weedy grass and walk up weatherworn porch steps that groan beneath my weight. My chest heaves, sweat's pouring down my face, and I ignore the mailbox that's overstuffed with junk and the package by the front door with Danny's name on it so that I can get inside and breathe cool air. This probably sounds mean—or at the least, lazy—but it's strategic. My mother has a responsibility to get her life together and it's sure as hell not going to happen if I keep taking care of everything for her.

The baby's crying, which is the first thing I hear when I walk inside. It's my sister's kid—Winter. She's eighteen months old and honestly, *crying*'s a generous word. What she's really doing is screaming. It's not like I blame her, either—that kid got a raw deal, straight out of the gate—but if this is what all babies are like, I seriously don't get how the human race has endured for as long as it has. There's a lot of shit to get off on in this world that doesn't create *that*. But hey, maybe more people than I realize do what my junkie of a sister did when Winter was just six months old, which is to ditch her screaming brat of a kid with her own mother before taking off for the last time and never looking back.

Her, I do blame, by the way. My mom should, too, although she's weak and she won't. From what I can tell, parents don't like to face hard truths about the kids they love, and anyway, avoidance is the path most people choose to walk, so it's hard to expect otherwise. Still, my mom's kind of an expert at the whole denial thing. Despite the fact that they both broke her heart, she continues to love my siblings. Endlessly. To this day, she contends that Darien's purpose in being born was to show her what love could look like. Danny, she says, was put here to show her the stars, what was possible. And me? Her youngest child? Well, my role to date has been to cause my mother unspeakable pain. This is what she tells me, at least, and I have yet to see evidence to the contrary.

Anyway, now that I'm home, I'd kind of like to do some avoiding of my own—like locking myself in the first-floor guest room, where I've taken to staying of late. Or else finding a way to get out of going to therapy tomorrow afternoon. It's a support group, actually, and it's totally unbearable. But I can't focus on that yet. Not when there's one more task standing in my way. The sooner I take care of it, the sooner I can move forward.

I venture deeper into the house, all shadows and empty space. Winter's screams grow louder, an echoing lament, but it's not until I get to the kitchen that I encounter my mother. Eating's not something either of us is doing a lot of these days, so it's not the first place I look, but I guess we've reached the point postmourning where no one's willing to stop by and help with the baby anymore. This means my mom is forced to feed Winter, along with other responsibilities she's loath to acknowledge, and I watch her from the doorway, half leaning against the beadboard wall. My mother's always been thin, but she's even thinner now in her grief and rage, a wraith hunched over granite while cutting up grapes with an effort that feels barely adequate.

Barely there.

I know I should go to Winter. My curly-haired niece is stuck in her jumper, which she's probably too big for, but she's given up jumping and she's just standing there, with her legs splayed and her fists clenched. Everything about her is furious, red with rage and scrunched up tight. A ball of need and primal longing. I could scoop her up or coo to her or otherwise distract her from her misery. It wouldn't fix the shit choices my sister's made or the fact that she's been left with a woman ill-equipped to handle her own basic needs, much less a child's. But it might get her to shut up for a few minutes.

It might help.

I don't do it, though. I hate myself for it, but I *can't*. I don't know how to say it other than that my heart won't let me. We're all fundamentally ill-equipped for life around here. This house is a blustering tornado of damage and dysfunction. So I do what I do best and ignore everything as I streak down the stairs to my mother's office on the basement level. This is where she runs the business side of her photography studio. Her partner's been handling almost everything since Danny died, and I couldn't tell you when my mother was last down here doing anything close to work. The air's musty, the curtains drawn, and while I've never liked this space to start with, I like it even less today.

Thankfully it doesn't take long to find what I'm looking for in the top drawer of her desk: a checkbook for the modest inheritance my father—who died before I was born—left behind in a trust for Danny and me. And let me acknowledge that I fully understand Darien's resentment and hurt over not being included in this—she wasn't his daughter, although he'd raised her as one—but it doesn't excuse any of what she did after. But maybe all pain comes home to roost, because I don't believe it was anything close to an accident that my sister abandoned her child with the mother she'd always rebelled against. The mother who'd always accepted her in the face of that rebellion. The mother who would never do the same for me.

Am I the worst or best of us all?

I don't have an answer to this question. At least not one I'm willing to acknowledge. What I do know is that I'm the one still here. This is what matters. The only thing. I truly believe this, which is how I'm so easily able to grab the checkbook and a pen and make it out to the club, the dues for the membership that will let me enter their gates and that I know I'll need. There's no way Coach Marks won't take me on once he sees me swim.

I turn to leave, check and pen still in hand. Returning to the kitchen feels like entering the darkest depths of despair—an execution room or an abattoir or some other form of purgatory lit by the lowest of expectations. I'm fairly certain my mother is crying. I'm fairly certain she wishes she were dead. But as always, her tears, her misery, fail to break my heart. So I walk over to her. Shove the check onto the counter and hand her the pen.

"Sign," I say gruffly.

And she does.

15.

Funds secured, I abandon the kitchen and lock myself in what's recently become my room, seeing as I don't go upstairs anymore. Too many ghosts float around up there, with no good reason for facing them.

I open my laptop and put on music to drown out Winter's crying. Kind of a shit thing to do, but I pick an album she likes and swear in my heart of hearts I'll hang out with her later. Kid deserves to be loved, and the way I see it, some is better than none. Next, I plug my phone into the wall to charge, sprawl my sweaty body across the pullout bed, and grab my training journal from where I left it beneath the nightstand.

Once the journal's in my hands, I roll on my back and flip to the page I've last marked. This is where I've been writing down my split progressions going back to the start of the calendar year. Freestyle's my best stroke, and like Danny, I'm built for middle distance: the 200 and 500 yd. events are where I excel, although I've competed in the occasional 1600. Most everything else that I keep track of on a daily basis is also written down in here: my workouts, weight, food intake, sleep output, how much I piss, shit, and jack off. Hell, I even make note of my mood, which is pretty much a joke, since when am I anything other than wrathful?

Well, comparing the bookmarked LCC results on my laptop screen against my own splits for the millionth time doesn't do anything for me in the mood department. In fact, seeing the reality of what I'll be up against is enough to make my hands grow clammy.

This past month has been understandably shitty in terms of training. Now that school's out, my only aquatic access has been the local community pool, which is a literal circus in the summertime. From open to closing it's packed with clueless families who crowd the deck with their giant wagons full of Goldfish crackers and swim diapers and foam noodles. To compensate, I've added hours of cross-training to my schedule: biking, running, weights. It's helped me maintain fitness, sure, but it's not the same as being in the water.

And it's definitely not the same as racing.

They say it takes twenty-one days to create a habit—a pattern of desirable behavior—which is fine and good, except it does nothing to help me figure out how to achieve what it is I want when it needs to happen in a fraction of that time. My desired behavior, by the way, is winning. Or, not winning, technically, which is hard to do without an actual race. But tomorrow I'll need to swim faster than I ever have in order to ensure that not only do I make Coach Marks's team, but that I'll be his top priority from here on out.

My focus, then, turns to building success instead of habit. After all, if past behavior is the strongest predictor of the future, then in order to do what I need to do tomorrow, it stands to reason that the best thing would be for me to do it before then, too.

16.

This is it.

My alarm goes off at two a.m. I sit up, bleary-eyed, yawning, but there's no hesitation. I'm still driven by urgency. I'm still aiming for perfection.

Swinging my legs to the floor, I start pulling on clothes and coming into consciousness, and I'm thankful I did my prep work before lying down to sleep last night. Everything I need is packed and waiting in my swim bag: my training journal, phone, a few water bottles, gels, a couple of sandwiches, extra clothes, plus all my regular gear: goggles, suit, fins, pool shoes, swim cap, and towel.

Desire's a hell of a drug. Adrenaline, too. Together they course through my bloodstream, fighting off any urge I might have to crawl back under the covers and give up on the realest dream around.

Quick glance outside. There's nothing but night, and seeing this pleases me. My favorite hours have always been the ones that come after midnight but before the dawn. I wish this were a moment I could savor—the start of the end or the end of the beginning—but time's march is relentless. I need to get going, so I grab my bag, pull it over my shoulder, and squeeze through my bedroom window to drop into a world spun from shadow.

My feet hit ground and I suck in air with a gasp. It's not cold out so much as *damp*, a late-night wetting of thick fog that soaks my lungs and chills my bones. Quiet footsteps. I pad my way from the side yard down the moss-covered driveway and out onto the street. I'll forgo the bike in favor of Danny's old car—his ancient Subaru, the one he called the Mink for her brown leather interior and dark brown paint. After he died, we had the car transported back from Los Angeles, and it's been sitting at the end of Lynnwood Court ever since. Pretty sure the neighbors aren't too happy about this, but it's not like they'd complain and besides, our overgrown yard is more of an eyesore. Anyway, it's not exactly legal for me to drive the Mink after hours—technically, my license is still provisional—but my mom's not awake to protest. And if she is, well, there's nothing she can do to stop me.

Sliding behind the wheel, I slip the key in the ignition and start the Mink's engine. Then I flip around for a radio station I don't hate before slowly pushing the car into first and easing off the clutch. The manual transmission is still new to me, but the car rolls forward with a low purr. There's no weariness inside me. No doubt or hesitation. Ahead of me is what I want and what I plan to get.

Screw the back roads. My initial plan was to keep a low profile, but now I crank the music up, roll the windows down, and point my ass toward the highway. The headlights bore through fog and the night air strokes my skin, a seductive slurp of power that works to sharpen my mind and heighten my senses. I love this, I realize, the fact that there are secrets only the night and I know. Not the moon or the stars.

Only the very darkness itself.

I'm someone else by the time I park the car. Or maybe something else. A creature winged and deadly. Fearsome, too. My actions run on autopilot and I park the Subaru off road in the bushes not far from where I stashed my bike less than twenty-four hours ago. Scattered beer cans, cigarette butts, discarded clothing, and worse dot the ground, glisten in starlight. These artifacts tell me others have been here, seeking the same privacy that I do, though for very different reasons.

As I leave her behind, I don't worry about the Mink getting towed or broken into. She's got too much magic in her for that to happen. Or maybe there's too much of the night sloshing around inside of me for me to care.

Car locked, bag slung over my shoulder, I slink deeper into the woods. The fog, the city lights all vanish beneath tree cover. Blackness is complete and the sole soundtrack I hear, other than my shoes crunching on fallen branches, is the faint hoot of an owl and the chirping song of the crickets. It's not until I reach the line of cyclone fencing and *Private Property* signs that I catch sight of the sky again. The fog's parted enough so that the moon's somewhat visible—a mere sliver, but I'll take it. God knows I need the guidance. I place both hands on the fence and begin to climb.

My nerves stay calm the whole ascent. It's true that security cameras could be filming my actions. It's true that there might be people who will know what I've done come morning. But these consequences are abstract, distant. This place doesn't have armed guards or around-the-clock security, and it's a paradox in a way. Lafayette's got money, but it's too safe a city to guard against crime in any actionable manner. Anyway, at the end of the day, I'm not a criminal. I mean, as a soon-to-be club member, I'm not really doing anything all *that* wrong.

Leg over fence. I twist and fall, knees to earth, and I've made it. I'm inside the club grounds. A quick check of my phone tells me it's 2:50 a.m., and a fresh whisper of wind urges me toward the aquatic center. When I reach the pool, there's no lock on the gate, just the spring-operated mechanism, and I push it open.

Walk right inside.

My heart rattles as I approach the water's edge. The pool at night's as pure as I've ever seen it. No lights. No people. Just inky motion, soft lapping.

A chilly bump and swell.

Breathing deep, I walk closer before kicking off my shoes. Bare feet on cold tile. I stare down at the unlit depths and see nothing but the same blackness above.

Come in, it whispers.

Join me.

My body obeys and my mind plays catch-up. Before I know it, I'm sliding off my pants, my boxers, wriggling free of my shirt. No one's here to watch and I have no bashfulness regarding my own nudity. Why would I? I know my flaws and greatness, in all their intimate detail.

Suit on, goggles in hand, I walk around to the deep end. I have approximately two hours to make up for four weeks of training, and I plan to condense my workout the way I condensed my sleep earlier. Quality over quantity. There's more to it than that, obviously. I'm well versed in the training principles of applied stress and adaptation and don't have time for either. But as any athlete understands, practice is more art than science, and more faith than reason.

The night wind rises. With a shake and shiver, I rub my hands down my arms and up my bare chest. Then I crack my neck, roll my shoulders, and shake out my lats, my hips, all the joints that hold my parts together. Finally, when I'm ready to go, I bend at the waist, tuck my chin to stare down the waiting darkness.

And dive.

18.

If there was ever a question, this is the answer.

My body cuts the surface, a sharp slice and splash, and then I'm under, rocketing through the frigid grip of the pool. It's tomblike down here, especially with the lights off, but I've never felt more at home or more like myself.

I read once that runners have bigger hearts than swimmers. This was explained as a function of physics and physiology; runners remain upright, requiring their aortic valves to work harder in order to push blood throughout their bodies. But I believe it's deeper than that. Swimmers are coldhearted and our anatomy reflects this. We thrill to the deep and the darkness, the danger of it all.

For two hours, I swim.

Back and forth.

Above and below.

19.

At the first hint of daylight, I crawl from the water, grab my bag, and flee indoors. It's time for recovery mode. Before I know it, 5:30 practice will be here and I need to get as much rest as I can before then.

Wrapping myself in a towel, I lie down on the carpeted changing-room floor with a pile of clothing under my head for comfort. It doesn't do much. Not to mention, there's no heat and my teeth won't stop chattering. Still I force my eyes shut. Sleep's not a real possibility and I have some vague concerns about spiders, but this state of stillness feels okay. It also lasts precisely fifteen minutes. This is when my alarm goes off, a noxious beeping that sets me cussing and fumbling for my phone.

Fifteen minutes until practice starts. Hopping up, I dash to the bathroom to piss, and when I return, my first priority is food. Hydration, too. Sustenance is what'll get me through the next few hours. I open my bag and shove down whatever I find as fast as I can find it: a sandwich, the gels, some sports drink. A whole bottle of water.

I'm still stuffing my face when the other guys walk in, a steady stream of sleepy eyes, long limbs, and broad shoulders. I watch them closely, my curiosity both abundant and bold, but for the most part, they're standard swim stock—a few appear to be a cut above ordinary, but that's it. I count eleven guys total, and a few look at me funny, their brows furrowed and questioning. But whether it's my presence they're curious about or the fact that my hair's already wet and my towel's damp, I don't know and don't care.

There are a couple faces I recognize, including Adam Fitzmaurice's. He's a year or so older than me and he's been getting a lot of attention of late. Local and beyond. He also swims free like I do, and fly, and I've heard his name mentioned in the same breath as my brother's. I have no clue if this comparison is warranted, but I do know this upcoming season will make or break him. He'll be going out on the national circuit, which will determine where he swims for college. If he's smart, however, he'll stay right where is—Danny's fate becoming a cautionary tale; don't stray from the man who made you—but seeing as Adam's best interest is in no way mine, I mostly hope he'll fail.

No one says a word. Everyone gets down to business, shoving their shit into lockers, checking their phones, popping their fucking zits in the mirror. And I get it. It's a weekday at dawn, that hazy space between night and day, truth and lies. A time when there's no point asking questions whose answers are more easily found in silence.

"Coach is here," someone announces, probably for my benefit, although I don't acknowledge this. The guys start the slow shuffle outside, and the adrenaline's back. I'm ready, more than ready, every muscle beneath my skin twitching and champing at the bit to get out there.

But I'm cautious and I make sure to bide my time. To not look too eager. I am also taken by surprise when one of the guys swims upstream and walks over to me.

"I'm Javier." He holds his hand out as a smile crosses his lips. He's on the younger side, still baby-faced and thin of chest, but I stare at him and I'm wary right from the start. It's definitely possible his friendliness is genuine, but the alternative puts me on edge, the notion that kindness is being weaponized as a means to disarm me. Seeing as I can't read this guy's mind or know his intentions, I'm left to trust my instincts, which tell me that the best defense is a good offense.

So this is the path I choose, and the reason I ignore Javier's waiting hand, his eager smile. Instead I get up, brush past him, and walk outside to join the rest of the team.

20.

Back on the pool deck, I try holding my own despite feeling off-balance. The moon, my one grounding element, is gone, and the sun, which is peeking over the distant mountains, casts long shadows and coats the world in an eerie pinkish light.

Wildfire light.

A rustle of dread awakens inside me, a queasy flapping of wings brushing against my ribs. I swing my arms and breathe deeply. It's just nerves, I tell myself. My body's way of reminding me that everything about today is important, although you wouldn't know it by looking at anyone else. Coach Marks is standing there with his stupid clipboard and his visor, and his expression is far from welcoming—more a mix of boredom and irritation. It's an expression I actually recognize. It wasn't until Danny was thirteen or fourteen that I stopped coming to watch him train, so Coach Marks isn't a stranger to me the way I am to him. But I want him to like me, and to this end, I follow the others' lead by huddling close, keeping my mouth shut, and listening as he launches into a lecture about the upcoming schedule.

This topic is of genuine interest to me. There are regional meets running throughout the summer, but September 25 is the cutoff for national ranking. It's imperative that I'm competing well ahead of this date in order to get my times down so that I'm ranked on the national circuit roster in the months leading up to the Olympic qualifiers. Because it's not that you *can't*, technically, qualify for the Trials with a verified time in an event that no one's ever heard of. It's that you won't.

The morning breeze bites. I rub my arms as Coach Marks shifts into some rah-rah cheerleading about "excelling in and out of the pool" and "fighting the good fight." It's seriously the worst and I don't know anyone who finds shit like this inspiring. There's not much I can do about it, though, so I let my eyes glaze over. It's likely everyone else is bored, too, because it's not long before I can feel their gaze on me—in a collective sense, all eleven of them. The group is sizing me up, from every angle, every direction.

I welcome this. Hell, I can take their scrutiny. Their skepticism. I can take anything, so long as I have secrets of my own.

"Gus," the coach calls out.

I lift my chin. "Yeah?"

"Glad you could make it."

"Glad to be here."

"You meet everyone?"

"Not yet."

He addresses his team. "This is Gus Bennett. He's been putting up some impressive times for Acalanes over in the state league for the past couple of years, which is why I've invited him here to swim with us this morning. So introduce yourselves, okay? Make him feel welcome."

There's a grumble of assent, more halfhearted than anything, but once they hear my name it's clear most of the guys know who I am without it having to be said explicitly. The worst part is the way the expressions on some of their faces slide from skepticism right into pity mode. Maybe a little sneering resentment, too—no matter the cost, they think I've been handed what they've earned.

"Let's get warmed up." Coach Marks rubs his hands together and there's no fanfare to it; we're supposed to jump in and start swimming. It's easy enough to follow along with what everyone else is doing—stripping off sweats, stretching muscles, testing the water temperature—but with twelve swimmers and ten lanes, I'm naturally one of the odd guys out. Someone's got to split with me and I know no one wants to. *"Let's be friends"* Javier's an easy enough target, but my standards are higher. I stroll over to Adam Fitzmaurice's lane. Give a terse nod.

Adam nods back but doesn't look up from adjusting his goggles. "Just stay to the right, okay? And don't ride my ass."

"What's your warm-up?"

"Eight hundred easy. Alternate free and IM. After that it's drills on your stroke of choice. You got fins?"

"Yeah."

"You swim free?"

"Mostly."

"Then follow what I do. I'm doing arm drills today. Working on turnover speed."

"And then?"

"He'll tell us." Goggles secured, Adam dives off the deck like he can't wait to get rid of me. His massive body vanishes beneath the surface, and with the light and sun and lane lines and the way my eyes work, it's as if he's disappeared completely.

I can't see him at all.

A cold hand on my bare shoulder makes me jump. I whip around and see that it's Coach Marks, showing me more affection than I can remember seeing him give Danny. My skin crawls at this realization. No one wants to be the do-over, and everything about this feels like a bad omen. Like I'm an actor on a movie set being forced to play a role I never wanted but signed up for anyway.

"Hey." I force a smile on my face.

"You doing all right?"

"Never better."

"Glad you're here," he says for the second time.

"Me too," I offer.

"After warm-ups, we'll be doing sprint sets, then some longer work at the end."

"Okay."

"Don't push unless I say so. I want to see *how* you work, Gus, not what you can do. There's a difference."

"Yeah, sure," I say, and well, I'm relieved he knows my name, but I'm barely listening. I can see Adam Fitzmaurice now. He's circling back through our lane, heading straight for me. My heart pounds and all I want is to be in that water.

Those sparkling depths.

Coach Marks releases my shoulder and I throw myself into the pool. I'm aiming for effortless, to match Adam stroke for stroke, but something's wrong. The water feels different than before. Where it previously contained me and held me up, it now collapses beneath my weight, allowing me to sink deeper.

And deeper.

I'm inches from the pool floor before I kick out hard. My muscles ache with the effort, and maybe I did too much earlier this morning, but that's no excuse for drowning. I just have to kick harder, fight more, finally breaking the surface to ease into my stroke.

Everyone else is far ahead of me, and the coughing that escapes my lungs does nothing for the impression I'm trying to leave. But screw this warm-up thing. I'm already ablaze—a combustible rush that needs no fanfare or flaming—and I push harder in an effort to catch up.

To make myself known.

I'm aware that this goes against Coach Marks's warning, but everyone knows there's no advantage to being left behind. Besides, my plan has always been to show, not tell, just like they say in English class. This means that no matter what Coach Marks says he wants to see from me, I absolutely, positively intend to give him all I've got.

21.

The impact's full force. A high-speed collision of bone on bone—a sharp crack of anguish that bursts right below my eye socket.

What the hell? I grunt, sputter, and lash out, swinging my arms every which way, trying to get whoever or whatever it is the hell away from me.

Someone shoves me, hands to chest, and I sink beneath the surface again. Clawing my way up, gasping for air, I hear the words "Fucking *asshole*," and it's *Adam*, I realize. He's pushing me off him, pushing me back, while treading water and glaring right at me. "I told you to stay to the right!"

"You're bleeding." Gripping the pool edge with one hand, I point to the cut on his lip. The red in the pool.

"No shit." Adam turns and swims for the wall, pulls himself out, and walks stiffly to the locker room. Coach Marks goes after him, which leaves me to assess my injuries on my own. I press down on my cheekbone, the space below my left eye. It's tender enough to bruise, but there's no blood, no lasting pain.

"What happened to Fitz?" The guy in the next lane over is staring at me. He's got both arms hooked over the lane line, water dripping from his nose.

"Don't know," I say casually. "Guess he must've hurt himself."

Dripping Nose Guy looks like he wants to ask more, like how and why and what did I have to do with it, but that's hardly a compelling reason to put my workout on hold. I push off from the wall. Start swimming again.

It sucks, knowing the coach's focus is elsewhere, and while my concern for Adam is sparse, I don't want him to be so badly hurt that it becomes some sort of issue. Also, I *did* run into him—I can admit that. So when the warm-up is over and we all get out of the water to stretch, I walk to where Adam Fitzmaurice is sitting on the edge of a lounge chair, towel wrapped around his waist, ice pack to his mouth, and mumble that I'm, like, really sorry or whatever.

"It's fine, Bennett," he says with a sigh. "Don't worry about it."

Well, I'm not *worried*. Not about him, anyway, although despite Adam's reassurances, the narrowed-eyes looks I get from the other guys tell me I'm not endearing myself to the rest of the team. But the feeling's mutual—nothing I've seen from any of them so far has impressed me—and besides, I've got other shit to think about.

Like what we're doing next.

The sprint sets are 15 x 100 m intervals of freestyle that we do in waves. Groups of three, which makes it kind of like a relay, except nothing about our combined times count and we have no common interest.

"I don't want to see max effort," Coach Marks barks. "Give me eighty-five percent, no more, no less. We've got fifteen rounds to get through, so this is about pacing and planning and swimming with your goddamn brain. You hear me, Vincent?"

Vincent, who's the shortest guy on the team and also the palest—his face and chest are dotted with freckles—nods vigorously.

"Good." Coach Marks calls out where he wants us to line up and how. I'm in the third, meaning last, wave, which makes sense even if it doesn't make me happy. He's got to know I'm dying to swim against his A team. To let them know how I stack up.

The first wave dives in.

I rub my arms and watch. I'm eager to see how they take it, if they hold back or if they think as I do—that there's no point in giving 85 percent effort.

That you might as well give zero.

The second wave takes off and I step to the edge, pressing my feet flat against the tile. Before bending down, I glance over at each of the other swimmers I'm lining up with and hold my gaze long enough that they all catch my eye.

I offer my most daring grin in return. The one that says *I'm hungry*.

And *I'll eat you up*.

Coach Marks shouts at us to get ready. The second wave's bringing it home, almost there, and I've got this. I dip my head and curl my lip to stare down the water, that moving, active force that lives to defy me.

I tense. Wait for the whistle blast.

We're off.

22.

I hit the water before anyone else does. A slick shot of power and gravity and utter desire. And you know what? I sure as hell don't sink this time.

I *fly*.

23.

Cool blue and checkered shadows. Beneath the water, I do my best to play it smart. The Turing machine inside my head works double time, feverishly calculating what pacing I need to hold to complete the full fifteen rounds. This is the work and art of distance sport: knowing how to hold back *just enough* at the start, so as not to risk crashing and burning later on in the homestretch.

But I *hate* holding back.

Everything about it feels wrong. Putting the brakes on goes against my instincts, and frustration batters at me like a hailstorm. What has it all been for, if not this? The hours I put in last night swimming laps beneath the light of the moon. The years I spent not daring to be half of what my brother was because I believed I wasn't worthy of glory.

Somewhere between my mind's eye and the whitewater view through my goggles floats my father's face. This probably sounds strange, considering I never met the man. Well, I've seen photos but our only communication before he died was filtered through my mother's womb and amniotic fluid, which isn't something I like to think about all that much. But maybe it's not so strange then that underwater is the place I feel closest to him, even though that's not very close at all. But he's the only person who ever cared about me, who's never let me down.

I make it through exactly three rounds of sprints before I wave the white flag. I can't do it, this holding-back thing. My skill is not in discipline but resistance. My heart pumps rocket fuel, and every time that whistle blows, I explode, pushing myself faster, harder, with every stroke.

My legs are jelly at the end of each interval, every time I drag myself from the water. Vincent, the pale guy with the freckles, actually has to pull me out after the tenth set. He holds me upright, while I shudder and struggle to catch my breath.

"Take it easy," he tells me, but I shake my head, wave him back.

"I'm good," I gasp. "I'm fine."

"Yeah, right," he says. "You know this isn't a race."

My head is spinning by the second-to-last set and I also start shaking in a way I can't control, so it's fair to say the warning signs are there. My body's failing, shutting down, but I have to keep going. I have to be better. Because *these* are the moments where greatness is born: not when you're ahead, but when all hope is lost.

What gifts have I given?

Who can carry me home?

It might seem the answers would be both nothing and no one. But that strobe light flicker of my father's face, the one I only know secondhand, is enough to remind me of what I have and will never let go of—that bitter swill of spite. For my shit life, my shit luck, and for everyone who's ever doubted me. Chest wheezing, stomach cramping, I drag myself to the edge of the pool for the final set. The whistle blows and I spring forward one last time, soaring out and over the pool with my hands clasped in front of me, my arms squeezed tight against my ears. The water rises to meet me and I cut the surface like a missile, shooting through the pool with a great swell and kick. Upon surfacing, I tear into my stroke, attacking the lane ahead of me with arms and rhythm and sheer goddamn will. I grunt and grit my teeth and rise above the pain, until finally, finally, I pull my way home, hitting hand to wall with a resounding smack.

I bob up as the other swimmers come in, which means I've beaten them. Ripping off my goggles, I squint up at the clock and register my time, although in truth it's meaningless. This isn't a race and I have no realm for self-comparison. But the impression, I remind myself. The impression's what matters. This is what they'll remember. So I haul myself out of the water with a mere toss of my head. No grinning or gloating. I do it like I expected nothing less.

Once on my feet, though, my stomach rebels. I try fighting it but there's no fight left in me. I make it to the grass before everything inside me comes up, not far from where Adam Fitzmaurice still sits nursing his bloody lip. Whatever. I don't care. I'm not embarrassed. Let everyone bear witness to what I'm willing to give. The way I see it, it's like taking Communion in church. You don't do it at home where nobody's watching, because demonstrations of devotion, well, they *mean* something.

Right?

"Jesus, man," someone behind me says in disgust. "Fucking hell."

24.

"So how'd I do?" Freshly showered and changed, I track down Coach Marks, finally locating him in his office. He's currently seated at a particleboard desk that's wedged inside a narrow sunlit space on the backside of the aquatic center. It wasn't easy to find this place. The office entrance is purposely hidden behind two wooden trellises lined with bougainvillea, and I hover in the doorway, loath to step all the way inside.

"How do you think you did?" The coach leans back and folds his arms behind his head. He's still got that tacky visor on and I can't help but wonder if he ever takes it off.

"I don't know," I say.

"Modesty doesn't suit you."

I shrug. "I think I was pretty good. Definitely hung with your guys."

"You didn't do what I asked you to. You pushed way too hard. You shouldn't be hurting yourself in a workout. Or anytime, for that matter. That's not progress. It's showboating and it's dangerous."

"I just wanted you to see what I could do."

"I'm aware of what you can do, Gus. I want to know if we can work together."

"We can," I say quickly. "I mean, I want to be a better swimmer. I want to be the best. And for that . . . I need you."

Coach Marks reaches for his coffee mug, takes a swig, and it's as if he wants me to believe he's actually giving the matter serious

thought. Like I don't know this is a game of dominance and sub-
mission that we've both agreed to play.

"So you talking with anyone?" he asks.

"Other coaches?"

"No, I mean a *therapist*. Someone professional. I want to know
that you're doing okay with everything."

This confuses me. "You want to know if I'm seeing a therapist?"

"Of course. Why wouldn't I?"

"Most coaches I know don't care about that sort of thing. It's
not like it matters once you're in the water."

"I'm not most coaches," he says. "And that's a factually inac-
curate statement."

My throat tightens. "Well, you don't have to worry. My mom's
making me see someone. Not one-on-one or anything, but it's a
support group for teens dealing with grief. I go every week. I'll be
there today, in fact."

He smiles. "I'm glad to hear it."

"Actually, it was the social worker who said it would be a good
idea. Not for grief reasons, necessarily, but because I'm the one
who—"

Coach Marks stares at me, awaiting the words I'll say next, but
now something's wrong and I can't speak. My throat's gone tighter,
like a tomb sealed shut, and being unable to finish my sentence is
suddenly no different than being unable to step inside his office.
There are some actions my body physically won't let me do.

"It's okay, Gus," Coach Marks says gently.

I nod. Look around. Hate myself for my weakness.

"What does your mother think of you being here?" he asks.

"I don't know," I manage.

"Maybe I should call her."

"Why?"

"It's a big commitment. Us working together. She should have
some input on the process."

"I'm sure it's fine. It's not like she doesn't know about the commitment."

"That's exactly why I should call her."

"She's already paid for my membership," I offer. "She knows what I'm doing."

"Oh, so you're a club member now?" he asks.

"I will be," I say. "I just have to pay up at the clubhouse. I'm actually going to go do that right now."

"So how'd you get in this morning?"

I freeze, thinking of the car stashed in the woods, the climb over the chain-link fence, but there's nothing distant about the coach's gaze right now. His brown eyes are sharp, focused, and knowing. The only response I'm able to give is a sheepish shrug.

"Uh-huh." His lips twitch as he turns away from me and back to his computer screen. "Practice is at six tonight. You find a legal way of showing up and I'll tell security to forget about what happened last night."

"Are you serious?"

"Always."

Backing out of his office, I turn and walk away with my heart pounding and a grin spreading across my face. I don't understand what it is that just happened. Not really. But I'm also not sure that it matters.

I'm coming back tonight.

25.

"Well, don't you look pleased with yourself." Adam Fitzmaurice jumps in front of me, blocking my path, right as I step outside the aquatic center and start heading for the clubhouse.

"How's that?" I stop. Adam looks completely different in street clothes. His hair's styled and he's wearing a collared shirt with pleated shorts and *Sperrys*, of all things. Somehow the effect on him is less rich-kid jock than church-group prude.

"You look like the cat that ate the goddamn canary." He says this like it's some big insult or something.

"Were you waiting for me?" I ask slyly, because it's totally clear he was.

Adam shrugs, pushes his black hair back off his forehead, and I just stare at him. He's older, barely, but we're the same height, same build, and we have the same sun-worn peeling skin. Yet he's the one who reeks of insecurity. It's practically wafting off him.

"How's your lip?" I venture.

"How's your stomach?"

"It's fine."

"Shouldn't eat before you swim."

"I'll take that into consideration."

The staring and the awkwardness between us stretches into uncomfortable territory. A woodpecker hammers at a tree above us and finally, Adam gives in and scrabbles for the high road. "How'd you like that practice?"

"It was okay."

"Just okay?"

"That's what I said."

"You coming back later? I saw you talking with Coach M."

"What if I am?"

"I'll assume that's a yes." Adam cocks his head. "You always this secretive about shit no one cares about?"

"You always ask questions about shit you don't care about?"

He gives a long sigh. "The guys didn't like you, you know."

"I know."

"They think you bought your way onto this team. Or that Coach M feels sorry for you. But that's not true, is it? I watched you today. You can't follow directions for shit, but you can swim."

"That's why I'm here."

"Well, I'm glad."

This doesn't make a lot of sense to me, but I grab for the opening offered. "Hey, can I ask you a question about the team? Or like, a few questions? This is all new to me."

"Sure," he says.

"Okay, first off, how much do you weigh?"

"One-eighty."

"And you're what, six-two?"

"Yup. Same as you, right?"

He's right, but I ignore this. "What other training are you doing?"

"Other than what Coach Marks has us doing?"

"Yeah."

Adam shakes his head. "Nothing. We do a total of nine practices in the water. And we hit the weight room at the club at least three times a week."

"Nine? That's it?"

"Quality over quantity. You can check it out on the website when you get access. Everything's on there."

"What about your nutrition, then? Do you see someone? Follow a plan?"

"You've got a lot of questions."

"There's a lot I want to know."

Adam considers this. "Give me your phone."

"What?"

"I'll give you my nutritionist's contact info. I see her twice a month. Coach M usually refers people to her, but seeing as you'll be sticking around, I can save him the hassle. I'll also send you the link to the info she's shared with me. It'll get you started until you can get in to see her."

I hand the phone over, screen unlocked. "Thanks, Adam."

"Call me Fitz." Adam—Fitz—types the info into my contacts and he's more relaxed now. His cheeks are flush, his dark hair's sticking up in a funny way, and a hint of a smile's dancing around his lips. He *enjoys* this, I realize, and the impression I get is that Fitz likes taking on this kind of mentor role. I guess I could be grateful, but there's an implication of hierarchy in this dynamic that I'm not eager to play into.

"You know, Gus," he begins, handing my phone back, and I steel myself because I know what's coming.

"Yeah?" I say.

"I'm real sorry about Danny."

And there it is. The elephant that's always in the room no matter how hard I try to shove its shitty ass outside. In response, I narrow my eyes. Lift my chin. "Are you?"

"Yeah. Of course. What happened . . . it was *awful*."

"Why?" I ask, as a thread of darkness begins to bore its way through me. "Why was it so awful?"

"What do you mean why?"

"I mean, without him here, isn't that better for you?"

Fitz's eyes go wide. "*No*. God. I looked up to Danny. He was awesome. I was at the Reno sectionals last spring, you know, as an alternate. I watched him swim that day and it was *hard*. For so many years, I've wanted to be like him. I mean, I still do. He'll always be one of my heroes."

Well, *this* makes me laugh. I can't help myself.

But Fitz is hurt—the wounded giver. "What's so goddamn funny?"

"Nothing's *funny*," I say, and the darkness inside me bores deeper still. "It's just sad, listening to you grovel over a dead guy. My brother was a loser. And a total asshole on top of that. Which means if you liked him so damn much, you're either an idiot or you're an asshole, too."

26

No good deed goes unpunished. This is how I think of Thursday afternoons and the fact that I have to spend every one of mine in a group therapy session over at the medical center in Walnut Creek. Not that I know what I'm being punished for, exactly, but it must be something pretty bad if it means being trapped in a room where other people are constantly talking about the horrible things that have happened to them.

Call me crazy or whatever, but I don't get what's supposed to be helpful about this. My personal theory is that whoever came up with the idea of a "grief group" was someone who hated talking about death and decided that if openly grieving people were forced to attend a special group where they had to listen to each other, then maybe everyone would keep their mouths shut in the first place. This is where punishment theory comes from, although that's not how the county social worker tried to sell it to me.

"Talking to someone after a traumatic event like this is important," she said during our one and only face-to-face meeting, in the living room of my mother's house. "Even if you feel okay now, symptoms can appear that disrupt your life later on. Like a delayed reaction."

"But I *did* talk to someone," I told her. "A counselor at my school. She didn't help me at all."

"Well, that counselor was worried about you."

"How do you know?"

"It was in her report."

I spent all of ten minutes with that counselor. I can't believe she wrote a *report*. "But isn't that illegal? Her telling you what I said? I'm supposed to have privacy or whatever."

"Not when there are safety concerns, Gus. You know that."

"What safety concerns?"

The social worker pressed her lips together. "Your mood and your reported panic attacks. Your lack of social support. Your refusal to talk about anything relating to your brother. Your own history, with . . ." She glanced at my arms and didn't say the rest but didn't have to.

My cheeks blazed. "That was a long time ago."

"Not that long."

"Well, it will be someday."

An unconvincing argument, and she won out in the end because going to therapy was never my choice to begin with. That's how everything goes when you're a teenager. Adults like to pander and pretend you have some say in your own life, but that just means it's your fault if any bad shit goes down. They'll take credit for the rest. Anyway, after that meeting, my mother was instructed in no uncertain terms to enroll me in some sort of mental health treatment for at least three months. She was allowed to choose something through her own insurance, a private care provider, or a program run through county services—whatever she felt was best.

What she chose was the cheapest and easiest option—a referral that came through my primary care doctor that I had to set up on my own. I was authorized for group treatment, which felt like low effort on the part of the insurance company. But I wasn't surprised. *Best* has never been a word my mother's chosen to associate with me.

Why would this be any different?

27

Walking into the med center's teen therapy room, with its shitty furniture, depressing posters, and tacky fluorescent lighting, I'm filled with the same low-grade nausea I always feel in this place. There are eight group members, including me, and what we supposedly have in common is someone in our immediate family dying in the last year in a traumatic manner. *Traumatic* is a subjective term, but trust me when I say everyone here qualifies. The stories I've had to listen to within these walls are *gutting*.

Anyway, rules are rules. I join the circle and take a seat. The group facilitator is this guy named Marco, who looks to be only a few years older than we are. He's a graduate student, which tells you how little value anyone places on the emotional well-being of traumatized teens. It's not like we're getting the field's best and brightest.

Like always, Marco starts off the session with a weekly check-in, and it's not long before my head is throbbing. This is the predictable result of being exposed to an endless recitation of vivid dreams and scarring memories of murdered fathers, cancer-struck mothers, drowned siblings, a cousin lost in a hunting accident, and a twin who dropped dead during cheerleading practice. The most disturbing story, however, is the one recounted by a fourteen-year-old girl who lost her mother and baby sister at an air show. Her family was sitting on bleachers in the warm Nevada sunshine when an antique plane fell out of the sky right in front of them. Apparently, it hit the landing strip and exploded, sending burning shrapnel spinning through the crowd with the force of a guillotine. The girl says that sound is what she remembers most and by this point—four weeks into our twelve-week group—it's safe to say it haunts each and every one of us.

"And, Gus?" Marco asks. "How's your week been?"

"Okay, I guess." Then, because I have to say something, "I'm swimming again. I swam today, in fact. A real workout."

"What made it real?"

I think about this. "I puked afterward."

"Gross." Air Show Girl, who's sitting across from me, makes a face.

"Sorry," I tell her, although I'm not.

"Wasn't your brother a swimmer?" she asks, playing with her hair. "Like, a really accomplished one?"

"He wanted to be."

"Oh, stop. He *was*. He was going to the Olympics. I saw a feature about him on CNN. He was really driven. Broke all kinds of youth records."

I fold my arms. "Not that driven."

"What do you mean?"

"I mean, my brother came close to qualifying for the US National Team last year. That's true. He was hoping to swim in the Olympics one day and a lot of people thought he would. I might've been one of them. But—look. I'll tell you what it takes to make the team and what he did to get there, and you decide if he was driven or not."

A hush comes over the room and Marco nods, gesturing for me to keep going. He's never heard me talk this much and even I don't know why I'm doing it. But I am.

I sit up in my chair. "Okay, the selection process for the US Olympic team is easy enough to understand in principle. The Olympic Trials are held ahead of the Games, and whoever swims fastest on that particular day is selected. That's it. No taking other results into account. Or previous experience. Glory goes to the winner, full stop.

"But to get to the Trials in the first place? Well, to do *that*, you have to swim under a set qualifying time. And not only do you have to swim a qualifying time, but you have to do it at a designated qualifying event, usually one of the premier national showdowns. And in order to swim in *those* events, guess what? You have to qualify, which means you've swum well enough and consistently enough on the regional circuit to be ranked at a level where you're allowed to compete nationally. And to get to the regional circuit and be ranked appropriately, you have to be good enough to be selected for an elite developmental team that has the means and interest to invest in you, as well as the vision to take you all the way to the top. That's to say nothing of all the years and competition and money it takes to join one of those teams.

"Oh, and one other thing: while the Olympic Trials are held every four years, the US National Team roster is set every year—these are the swimmers who train with the national coach and represent the US out on the international circuit. It's similar to the Olympic qualifier, except that there are usually a handful of events that are designated for consideration. Any swimmer fast enough to get on the circuit has a shot, and that's what Danny was aiming for when he qualified for the Reno sectionals in April."

"Did he go?" Air Show Girl asks.

"Yeah. But before that, he left his longtime coach in Lafayette to swim for UCLA, with their coaches."

"Why?"

"I don't know," I say honestly. This is one of the bigger mysteries surrounding Danny. If he'd made the national team, he wouldn't have been swimming on the college circuit anyway, so the shift was abrupt. And somewhat unprecedented. "He must've thought he'd do better there. And he did, actually. He was favored heavily to make the national team. I didn't get to watch him compete, but my mom went, and I don't really know what happened. My sense is that Danny knew he'd fucked up a good thing by leaving his coach and he let that get to him. After all, if you fuck up one thing, who's to say you won't fuck up more?"

The girl frowns. "But you said he was swimming better."

"He was. Until he wasn't. My brother got out there on that stage he'd spent his whole life chasing and he choked. Came in fifth in both his events, well over his best times. After, he acted like it didn't matter, like winning wasn't the goal and just being there was enough. All that humble shit people say but never mean. Then a month later, well, you know . . ."

"I'm sorry," she says.

"Don't be."

"Well, I am."

"Well, I'm not."

Air Show Girl bites her lip, and there's anger in the way she's looking at me. Or else disgust. "You don't mean that."

"I do," I tell her. "I absolutely mean it and no one ever believes me. But I'm sick to death of everyone saying my brother was a hero just because he was good at swimming. Ultimately, it didn't matter to anyone but him. It's not like it's some noble calling requiring endless selflessness and sacrifice."

"You don't think it's a sacrifice to give up things you want?"

"Not when it's for your own gain. Not when what you want is for everyone to see you win and to be recognized for that. That's not *sacrifice*. It's ego. It's arrogance. I mean, look what happened when Danny lost. He chose to die rather than live with his failure and left all this bullshit for the rest of us to deal with." I glare around the room. "What's more selfish than that?"

28.

I was barely seven when I realized my brother was going to be a champion. This memory is as vivid and visceral as any other. Danny, who was nine, was already swimming competitively. He'd moved up from the local rec league to a bigger swim team that trained in Orinda and on the weekend traveled for meets that were as far away as Santa Cruz and Sacramento.

Usually, I stayed home while Danny swam. He'd go off with our mother—sometimes overnight—while Darien looked after me. My sister was sixteen at this point, and if she wasn't happy about having her baby brother around, she did it for the gas money and rarely complained. For the most part, I didn't mind tagging along with her and her friends. They were feral creatures, preferring to stay outside and gather in open spaces like Briones Park, with its thousands of acres of wooded trails and secluded hillside. Once there, they'd drink beer and smoke weed and play acoustic guitar and no one cared at all what I did. Roaming, ever restless, I tried climbing every mountain I found, scaling red rock and clay and soaring to terrifying heights until my sister hollered at me to get my ass back down. I never wanted to stop; there had to be something higher, something worth reaching. I was sure of it.

Then one day Darien left home and didn't return. This was the first time she ran away, but not the last, and my mother had no choice but to bring me along with her to one of Danny's meets in San Jose. She complained the whole time and acted put out and I didn't even want to go because I knew I'd hate it. What could be more boring than watching someone swim back and forth in a man-made cube of water? Not to mention, I really couldn't imagine Danny was any good. My mom was always bragging about him to anyone who would listen, but Danny was a different kid back then—twitchy, nervous, and plagued with headaches, rashes, and other ailments that required visits to specialists and frequent blood draws.

But in the pool, this all changed. My brother leapt from the blocks with a power I didn't know he had, streaking for the far side against a field of bigger boys. Watching him fight for dominance, I went crazy. I cheered and yelled and stamped and even hugged my mother when he won. She hugged me back, which was a surprise. I couldn't remember a time when she'd done that. But she held me close, her cheeks pink, her heart pounding, my nose filled with the scent of her lavender lotion. In her arms, I melted a little, and finally, I understood what might be at the top of the goddamn mountain.

Everything.

The meet ended. We tried to get to where the team was gathered, but it was so crowded, my mother and I couldn't move from the bleachers. Eventually the head coach made his way over to where we were and started talking my mom's ear off about Danny's future. What kind of commitment my mother would have to make and what that would mean for our family. He listed off everything she'd have to pay for: private lessons, a private trainer, getting Danny on a more competitive circuit that would have him traveling all over the western states. It sounded like it would cost a ton.

She agreed to everything without even asking Danny. She ignored my tug on her arm when I grew bored, and I started looking around for Danny, hoping to catch sight of him in the crowd. And there he was. No longer awkward or sickly, my brother stood on a podium, holding a trophy in the air and posing for photos. You could see his destiny in that moment. It was evident in his triumphant grin, stretching from ear to ear, and in the water dripping from his dark curls. The rest of his team lingered in the shadows, unnoticed, and when Danny finally turned and walked toward the locker room, I caught the way his teammates looked at each other. They *hated* him, I realized.

Every last one of them.

29.

My destiny, it would appear, is to be eternally pissed off. Even now, as I step into the same gilded paradise Danny once ruled and then squandered, nothing comes easy for me.

I do my best to fit in, adjusting quickly to the practice schedule and showing up to the club early almost every day. This gives the team the impression I'm a morning person, but the truth is that sleep is more work than it's worth these days. Too much leaves me jumpy, short of breath, with my nerves wrung dry by a dream residue that seeps into my waking hours. I try harder with food, but satiety's not a natural state for me. It may not be optimal from a physiological standpoint, but I perform best when both underfed and overworked. Hunger sharpens me, I find.

Struggle defines me.

Endearing myself to Coach Marks is likewise a challenge. I employ different tactics, ranging from rote obedience to ass kissing to self-deprecating jokester. Nothing works. He simply treats me the way he treats all his swimmers, barring Fitz, who's his favorite. After a few weeks, in an act of desperation, I try the one thing I shouldn't—being myself.

"Why're we only doing nine workouts a week?" I blurt out at the start of evening practice. It's a sweltering Thursday in early July. One of those endless days where even darkness can't beat back the heat and the mosquitoes seem sapped of energy, too lazy to bite or swarm. "We should be doing more."

Coach Marks squints at me. "You got a problem with the way I run my team, Bennett?"

"I've got a problem with the way you don't," I counter.

Some of the guys laugh at my response. They think I'm making a joke, which says more about them than it does about me. But Coach Marks knows I'm serious.

He knows I always am.

He tugs the brim of his visor. "My goal is to push you when you're in the water and make sure you're recovering well when you're not. To keep you healthy. To keep you injury-free. And to keep you improving."

"So one size fits all?"

"That's not what I'm saying."

I tilt my head. "What are you saying?"

"That if you're swimming for me, you're following my program. And I believe in intensity. I want you doing better workouts. Not more."

"That's it?"

"What else could there be?"

"You make it sound like I shouldn't ask questions. Like I should just be following orders."

"I never said that. But this is a relationship based on trust—which goes both ways, remember—and if you don't trust me or the way I work, then you shouldn't be here."

"Yeah, whatever," I mumble because I can feel the tide turning against me—no one's laughing anymore. But it's not like I'm full of shit. Training isn't a religion. It's not a matter of faith or wanting something to believe in. It's about evidence, which I have plenty of. It's all written down in my training journal. And yes, I *have* seen improvement in my times. It'd be hard not to, considering I didn't have access to a real pool or regular workouts for more than a month.

But it's not enough. Not even close.

My brother didn't leave me anything when he died, but I found *his* training efforts and split times going back years logged in a spreadsheet on his phone. I printed it out and currently have it pinned to the wall in my room for comparison to my own, and the story his notes tell is that not only did Danny improve faster from where I am now, but he trained *harder*. A lot harder. In fact, three years earlier, he was at this exact club in this exact same pool doing twelve-plus workouts a week—that's doubles every weekday plus two workouts a weekend, not even counting dry-land training.

Next practice, I arrive early and I bring with me the evidence I've collected. I try showing it to Coach Marks as he pulls the covers off the diving pool and checks the filters. I have everything he needs to see. Screenshots of then and now. The difference is obvious and undeniable.

"What's your point?" he asks, like the point isn't right in front of his face. But he can't be bothered to do more than glance at my phone. Part of the pool cover gets twisted and he turns away from me, reaching into the water to get it straightened out before reeling it the rest of the way in.

I pace behind him while he works. "My point is that *this* is what you did with Danny when he was my age. Look how many reps he was doing. Plus all those intervals and progressive sets. It was *working*. His times dropped to national level in a matter of weeks. But I'm capable of more and I'm not working half as hard as he was, which means there's no way I can improve at the same rate! It's not possible."

"Okay," he says, still not looking at me.

I shove my phone back into my pocket. "So which is it: are you sabotaging me on purpose? Or is it that you don't think I'm good enough to work that hard?"

Coach Marks turns and shakes water from his hands, flinging the drops back toward the pool in a useless act of conservation. "I'm not sabotaging you."

"You're sure about that?"

"I also think you're plenty good enough."

"Then why?" A plaintive edge overtakes my voice in a way I hate but can't help. "I can do it. I know I can."

"Because you're not the same person as your brother. You're a different swimmer than he was. And I'm different, too. I'm not the same coach I was back then."

"Well, why the hell not?" I ask.

"Gus . . ."

"What?"

Coach Marks steps back from the pool, his work, and looks around. "Why don't we sit and talk about this. Somewhere private."

I'm instantly wary. "Why do we have to sit?"

"You seem . . . agitated."

Uh-uh. No way. This is my cue to back off because what he's offering is the last thing I want. Sympathy and sad eyes and all that mealymouthed bullshit won't do me any good. It won't do anything but inject a belief in Coach Marks's head that I'm weak. That I'm not cut out for this.

I wheel around and march off, heading for the locker room while muttering some excuse about needing to get changed. The worst thing, though, is the betrayal of my own heart. I can't explain it, but it takes everything I have to walk away from Coach Marks. To keep from running back and confessing that the only thing I want from him is what I've always needed. From my mother. From Danny. From everyone I've ever known.

More.

30.

After watching Danny dominate at the meet in San Jose, I remember asking my mother if I could learn to swim the way that he did. But she said no. Just right off the bat.

"But why not?" I whined. "I might be good. Like Danny is. Maybe even better."

My mother scowled. "Do you think Danny would like that?"

"I don't know." I couldn't understand why this would matter. Danny didn't like a lot of things and most weren't predictable.

"I don't know," she repeated back to me in a mocking tone. "You don't know anything, do you?"

"Never mind," I said.

She wouldn't let it go. "You want everything, don't you? You think you should get everything that pops into your stupid little head."

"I said never mind!"

"There's only one of me." Her voice spiraled louder. "Did you ever stop to think about that? Did you ever stop to think about *my* needs and if I had the time to drive two kids all over the goddamn place every day, every weekend? I deserve a life, too, you know."

"I *know*. I never said you didn't!"

"Oh, just shut up already, would you?" She grabbed my arm and pulled me with her through the crowd in search of Danny. "Your brother's worked hard for this and he doesn't want you copying him. It's selfish to want what you haven't earned. Don't you know how to do anything for yourself?"

"Fine." I sulked and felt angry and didn't dare ask again. But inside, I was undeterred. My mother didn't know what I could do because she didn't know anything about me. I was a swimmer. Or I would be. This was a truth that had awoken inside me while watching Danny race. My body belonged in that water just as much as his did. Nothing else would tame the fire roaring through my heart, my mind on a daily basis.

Well, ten years later, it seems Coach Marks won't be the one to tame those flames, either. He can't be, not if he won't put me in the pool and push me to train the way my brother did. Not if he wants me to sit and talk about my feelings more than he wants me in the water. So in the aftermath of trying to get him to up our training intensity, I do what I should've done earlier; I plot my own path to glory.

This takes cunning on my part. And more than a little creativity. After all, breaking into the country club every night isn't a viable option—not if I want my arrest record to stay clean—so I once again dip into my dead father's trust fund, this time via a passable forgery of my mother's signature, and use the money to obtain a second membership at a swim club eight miles outside Lafayette near Clayton Valley, located in a semirural area. No one at this club knows who I am. Honestly, the place is barebones: the pool's on the smaller side—twenty-five meters long and only five lanes—but unlike our city rec pool, there are no swim teams or lessons. It's purely for lap swimmers and the occasional family outing. Best of all, there are no distractions like golf courses or country club soirees. There's a pool. A shower. A small strip of grass.

That's it.

From there, it's easy to get into a routine. A little more forgery gets the Mink's registration renewed under Danny's name, and with my brother's driver's license stored in my wallet in case of emergency, I start showing up at the Clayton Valley pool around ten every evening on the days we're not doing doubles. This is late enough that all the families and sunbathers have left but not so late the place is closed down. I have until midnight to do my thing. Occasionally I run into other lap swimmers, but they don't bother me. Once I'm in the water, in my lane, there's nothing on my mind but the rhythm of my body casting its own wake.

Soon, I'm getting in thirteen workouts a week. It's not long before I feel the difference in my strength. My speed. Coach Marks can see it, too. My progress is right there on his stopwatch and I've never had my times drop like this. Even swimming for my high school team, we never got enough time in the water. Too many scheduling demands and conflicts. But other than babysitting Winter, going to group, and avoiding my mother, my life now revolves around one purpose and one purpose only, and the improvement I'm seeing pushes me to work harder. I'm diligent about hitting the gym, putting on muscle, and while my sleep's still shit, I vow to get better with eating. With making sure I get what I need, right down to the fucking gram.

Whatever it takes.

I'm willing to give.

31

"Not only will our group be ending this week, but we're into August already and that means school will be starting up again. This is a big transition. Two transitions, really." Marco pauses and sits back to let the impact of his words sink in.

Glancing around the therapy room, I understand what he's doing but I'm doubtful the impact he's anticipating is actually happening. No one wants to purposely make him feel useless, but the primary emotion I'm reading off the other group members is relief. But that, as Marco is so fond of saying, may just be my own projection.

"Lynette, how are you feeling about all of this?" He stacks the odds in his favor by asking the one girl in the room who's openly weeping. Thirteen years old, Lynette Kernfield's a mousy thing with knotted hair and bony shoulders. Eight months ago, her beloved baby brother drowned in the bath while she was supposed to be watching him, and I mean, *fuck*. What can you say about something like that other than the world is a shitty place littered with the offal of human suffering? I don't know the girl or her family in any context other than this room, but I'm pretty sure I've been more traumatized by her brother's death than my own. We all have. Anyway, Lynette is almost always weeping, and her sorrow is the kind that makes you wish those memory-erasing technologies you see in movies were real.

"I don't know," Lynette says in response to Marco's question about her feelings. "But I'm looking forward to school. I'll be in ninth grade this year. High school. I love science and I'll get to take biology where we do real lab work. I want to do debate, too."

"Wonderful." Marco beams but everyone else stares at the floor in collective horror. This time I'm positive they're thinking the same thing I am, which is some variant of *For the love of Christ, please let everything be okay for Lynette. Let her be happy and not have ninth grade be the shit storm of misery we all know it will be. Don't let asshole boys call her a cunt or a baby killer and don't let rich-bitch girls who only care about their image shun her for her awkward mannerisms or throw tampons at her in the shower like in* Carrie. *Just please, for once, don't let the lamb be eaten by the lion.*

"Gus?" Marco says. "Any thoughts about your future? How's swimming coming?"

"Could be better."

"How so?"

I shrug. "I'm working my ass off and my coach still hasn't put me on the roster for any of the meets this summer. None of the good ones anyway."

"You ask him why?"

"I'm trying not to."

"Why would you do that?"

"The more I ask, the less likely he is to say yes. That's what he says anyway, so now I'm trying persuasion by silence."

"Sounds like superstition," Marco says.

"Yeah, maybe."

"What about school? You looking forward to that?"

"I don't even know when it starts."

"Will there be people there who will want to talk about your brother?"

I fold my arms. "Nobody there knew him. He mostly did online schooling from eighth grade on. Besides, Danny hated school. Thought it was a waste of time."

"How so?"

"He said the only purpose of our education system was to teach us not to question why we were there in the first place."

"Sounds like something you would say."

"I guess. It's probably the only thing Danny and I had in common."

"Besides swimming, you mean."

"Right," I say.

Marco gives me a funny look before moving on to someone else and I'm left feeling more than a little confused. It's true that I'm not looking forward to school, but I'm not sure how the swimming connection between Danny and me slipped my mind. It's usually all I think about. Anyway, everyone gets a chance to speak and near the end of the session we're forced to do some dippy closing exercise where we all walk around with pens and pieces of paper taped to our backs. Marco instructs us to write a personalized message of gratitude to the other members, along with a positive memory of their contribution to the group. It's basically the worst and I can't fathom that there are people in the world who enjoy contrived sap like this.

But Lynette starts crying again, so while I'm shit for gratitude, I do my best and rack my brain for memories of these people I hope to never see again. Some of the moments I come up with are funny—like the time Marco asked Anya the Air Show Girl if not having nightmares anymore about the accident would be like experiencing the loss all over again, and she replied, "Who the hell cares? I just want my beauty sleep." But before we can read the messages written to us, Marco plucks the papers off our backs and stuffs them into individual envelopes while promising to hand them out as we're leaving.

"Can't we just read them now?" someone calls out. "I want to know what you assholes said about me."

"Patience," Marco insists. "Doing it this way allows you to leave the group with something tangible. A transitional object, if you will."

"Like a teddy bear?" I add wryly.

He sighs, exasperated. "I mean, if that's what you want it to be."

32.

Later, I stand in my bedroom with the A/C blaring and pull the sealed envelope Marco handed to me out of my backpack. My fingers run along the sharp edges as my mind swims with memories of a different unopened message—one I came across back in May while rummaging in the Mink's glove compartment the week after the transport service returned her to us.

For reasons that will never be made clear, Danny abandoned his car and his college and flew home to die on a plane ticket he bought with our mother's credit card. Maybe it was meant to be the ultimate fuck-you. Sticking her with the bill for his final travel expenses. Although if that's the case, I don't know what he had to be so mad about. She would have willingly paid for the damn thing if he'd just asked. Probably would've tied the rope for him, too.

That's how much she loved him.

The envelope I found in the glove compartment wasn't like the one I'm holding now, which is just a cheap Staples knockoff, already creased and worn with minimal handling. The one in Danny's car was larger, thicker, and made of creamy card stock. Its heft gave it importance, and an address I didn't recognize was written on the front. No name, though, but the handwriting was definitely Danny's. I could tell right away. But seeing as the message inside wasn't meant for me, I didn't think to open it. I just shoved the damn thing back where I found it, and as far I know, it's still there.

Well, the message I'm holding now *is* meant for me. It's got my name on it, and I can still feel the fading sensation of other people's hands scrawling their memories of me onto my back. But I don't bother opening this envelope, either. I force it into an over-crowded desk drawer, alongside a bunch of other letters and junk and trash I don't have the energy to deal with.

Then I shut the drawer. Tight. I guess you could say I have a thing for delayed gratification and that this is the reason I'm not interested in reading what the group wrote about me or what memories they chose to share. It would be an accurate account of who I am and what I'm like.

But more accurate would be to say I simply don't care.

33.

"You're quiet tonight," Coach Marks tells me a few weeks later at the end of evening practice. Reluctant to leave the pool, I've stayed to get a few more laps in while he watches. Now sitting on the tiled edge by the steps with my feet still submerged, I lean my head against the railing and watch as he uses the skimmer to pull dead leaves out of the pool. A few drowning spiders.

"Aren't I quiet every night?" I ask, although I know this isn't true. I run my mouth all the time, but it's not like he ever listens. It's not like anyone does.

"Hey, how was school today?" he calls from where he's standing and shaking the wet leaves onto the grass. "You've been back for a week now, right?"

"Next question," I call back.

"I'm serious."

"I didn't go today."

Coach Marks frowns and sets the skimmer down. After brushing his palms off, he comes back over and settles beside me on the pool's edge. "Why not?"

"I don't know."

"You don't know?"

I close my eyes. The urge is there to say something about wanting to do online learning like Danny did when he was on the traveling circuit. But it wouldn't come out honest. It would sound like I *want* something from him. Which I do. I want him to put me on the roster, to let me race. Only I can't ask for this directly, because I'm supposed to prove I trust him.

Which I don't.

"That bad, huh?" he asks.

"I guess."

"Sorry to hear it."

"That's okay."

"Will I see you this Friday night?"

I open my eyes. "What's happening on Friday?"

Coach Marks offers me a rare smile, the one that says I'm not fooling anyone—least of all him. "It's the dedication ceremony for the scholarship that the Brownings are starting in Danny's name. I know you know this."

"Whatever." My feet turn circles in the water.

"It'd be nice if you came," he says.

"Would it?"

"It would mean a lot to your mother."

My feet turn faster. "How would you know?"

"She told me."

I jolt, quickly pulling my feet from the water and bringing my knees to my chest. The image of Coach Marks talking with my mother about me, about *anything*, isn't something I can deal with.

"You're upset," he says.

"I don't like people talking about me behind my back."

"She's your *mother*."

"Maybe you should remind her of that."

Coach Marks sighs. "I know this can't be easy, but I really think it would be good for you to come on Friday. There's so much more to this sport than what you do in the water, and it wouldn't hurt to let people get to know you a little. To let some of us in and help you get through this."

My eyes widen and I stare at him with the sudden understanding that he really and truly believes my reluctance to go to the dedication ceremony is because it might be too painful for me. That I'm still in the throes of grieving my brother's death and that the only issue is that I'm too repressed to say this.

"You can't keep hiding forever," he adds.

"I'm not hiding! You're the one who won't let me—" I snap my jaw shut before I can say more.

"You're not exactly social."

"I didn't know that was a prerequisite for swimming."

"It's not, but . . ."

"But what?"

"It'd be nice to have you there."

"*No.*" I grip my knees tighter. "It wouldn't."

Coach Marks is quiet for a moment. "Maybe you could help me understand what's going on with you. Because I really feel like I'm missing something, Gus."

"You shouldn't be," I mutter. "It's not like I didn't tell you on the first day I came here or anything."

"What did you tell me?"

"That I'm not sad about what happened to Danny! That the only thing that matters to me is being better than him. That I want to make his name, his legacy, everything about him, disappear!"

"You said that?"

"I said I wanted him compared to me."

Coach Marks nods and takes a deep breath. "Okay. Yeah, you did. I guess I thought that was your competitive nature speaking."

"No."

"So I take it you didn't like him very much."

"For good reason."

He doesn't answer. I'm pretty sure he has no idea what to say. Coach Marks isn't just going to the dedication ceremony, he's giving the main speech at it, and I'm guessing the bottom line is that we don't have a whole lot in common on this topic.

"Did *you* like him?" I ask, because I have to know. "Danny?"

"Yes," he says, after a moment. "I did. I still do. I liked him a lot, and I wish . . . I wish we'd had more time together. I wish I could've been there for him."

My shoulders droop, but what did I expect? None of this is a surprise. Still, it's the *wistfulness* in his voice that gets me. I hate hearing it, and even the word itself sounds like remorse. *Wistful.* A wish long gone and never granted.

"Does that make you uncomfortable?" he asks. "Knowing how I really feel?"

"Not at all," I say tersely.

"Then what it is? What's wrong?"

I roll my head back. "It makes me think less of you."

34.

A funny truth: Danny's the one who taught me to swim in the first place.

It happened during the summer after Darien ran away from home that first time. Danny and I spent eight weeks at a city-run day camp while our mother worked. We needed full-time care and even Danny's elite athlete status couldn't get him out of going. He wanted to go, though, which surprised me and also contradicted my own emotions. I didn't want to be outside all day with strangers. But Danny, filled as he was with his newfound confidence, said it would be a chance for us to make friends and to have a little freedom in our lives for once.

The camp met at the local reservoir. There were fields and trails and a rocky shoreline with a designated swimming area marked by ropes. Not knowing how to swim, I rarely ventured into the water, occasionally daring to wade in the marshy spot lined with reeds where the youngest children chased tadpoles and dragonflies in water no deeper than their knees. I wore my shorts and sandals when I did this rather than incur my mother's anger by asking for swim trunks.

Danny was the one who forced the issue. He gave me a pair of his old trunks and told me he'd teach me to swim.

"I don't know," I said.

"Everyone needs to know how to swim," he said. "It's a matter of survival."

"Mom said I couldn't. She was really mad."

"Forget about that. She doesn't care if you swim."

"How do you know?"

"She's just mad you asked about it. It's not the same thing."

"Fine," I said, because if Danny was an expert on anything outside of swimming, it was definitely our mother. She doted on him in ways that didn't make sense. Like when he was really young and had screaming tantrums and refused to go to school, she'd say he had separation anxiety, meaning separation from her.

Her cure back then was to baby the hell out of him. I remember standing in the kitchen, watching her warm milk for hot chocolate and make brown sugar toast, while she cooed to Danny what a *brave* boy he was. I'd never heard of Pavlov's dogs at that point in time, but even my childish brain could understand that Danny was being rewarded for his fears. But I didn't dare challenge her methods. Danny was fearful, I'd been told, because his father had died when he was little, and that was a terrible, tragic thing.

Well, my father had died, too, but I wasn't fearful. I was something else. So when we got to the day camp, I put my suit on and let Danny lead me into the reservoir's chilly depths. Here, he taught me to float and kick and blow bubbles. I took to it as quickly as he promised and by the end of the summer, I was swimming to the raft and back. Danny even had me racing against the other eight-year-olds and I beat them every time. I'd haul ass out and back, returning to the shore with my chest heaving, only to clamber to my feet and sprint up the rocky beach so that I could see my brother's grinning face.

"You're awesome, Gus!" he'd say, before high-fiving me, and I loved it. His praise. His approval. His friends would cheer, too, which only pushed me to swim faster, and when summer was over, Danny worked some sort of different magic and convinced our mother to let me join his swim team in Orinda. She resisted at first, but he reminded her that we'd be there together. It wasn't like it would make extra work for her. Just the opposite; she wouldn't have to find childcare for me now that Darien was out of the house and who knew where.

That year was a whirlwind time. If not rags to riches, it was like moving from the cargo hold up to first class. My mother remained chilly toward me—she always was—but I thrived on the swim team, and for the first time, I was eager to be a part of something. I was good, too, but more than anything I was proud to be Danny Bennett's little brother. Everyone knew who he was and what he would someday do.

For a while there, Danny was *my* champion and the feeling was almost mutual. That was the best part, and it was as if Danny suddenly saw me as an extension of him. A winner by proxy. Not only did my success up his stock, but he liked the attention he got for caring about his kid brother. To a point. I made it through one full season on the Orinda team and by the end I was winning everything in my age-group. I even broke a couple of Danny's U-10 records. My downfall, of course, was being dumb enough to boast about this and the fact that my coach had dubbed me "the future of the league."

That was that. The season ended and by that I mean Danny abruptly stopped speaking to me or acknowledging my existence. A few weeks later, my mother sidled up while I was watching television. She plopped down on the couch beside me and with the smuggest look I'd ever seen announced that our family wouldn't be returning to the Orinda club the following year.

"Why not?" I asked.

"Danny's been accepted to the Lafayette Country Club. He'll be training under Colin Marks from now on."

"Who's that?"

She laughed. "Only the best coach in the country. Or one of them."

"He's going to coach Danny?"

"That's right."

"Oh," I said, but my mom lingered. She didn't get up and leave or say she was sorry. Instead she stayed right where she was, her fingers tapping away on the sofa's armrest. She stayed there and she kept smiling and staring and waiting for me to ask what was going to happen to me and if I could swim at the country club with my brother and the very best coach in the country. But I didn't. I refused to give her that satisfaction.

Besides, I already knew.

35.

Friday night rolls up and the closest I get to the dedication ceremony is watching my mom get ready for it. It feels a little masochistic, but there's also an air of absurdity to the whole thing. Not only is my mother getting all dressed up, but she's even having her hair and makeup professionally done. Like it's the Oscars.

A few of her friends drop by for drinks before heading over, and I know they mean well. Plus it's good for her to have a social life and people who care about her. She shouldn't be moping around all the time like she usually does. But it seems morbid to turn the occasion into a party. Maybe that's just me, though, because I hate that any of this is happening at all.

In need of distraction, I focus my efforts on helping Winter, who's also going. We're standing in the downstairs bathroom together, and she's wearing a sparkling green dress that has her resembling a bright-eyed leprechaun. It's cute, I guess. Green was Danny's favorite color so it's a good tribute, but I happen to know that Winter's favorite dress is one with sunflowers printed all over it.

"You sure you want to wear this one?" I ask.

"Uh-huh," she says.

"Let me do your hair," I say.

Winter knows the drill. She sits on the stool in front of me while I work on detangling her curls in the mirror. I don't know how to do much more than that, but I'm careful not to pull and her dark hair ends up soft and bouncy.

"What do you think?" I ask.

She slides off the stool, then turns to grab my leg. Staring up at me with eager eyes, she beckons me closer.

I squat to Winter's height. "What is it?"

Smiling, she takes the brush from my hand and begins to groom my own head. The bristles are sharp and she's not at all gentle, but reciprocity is a rare occurrence in my life. I can't help but milk the moment for all it's worth and stay still until my hair is styled into a shape that leaves me looking like a long-lost Kennedy cousin.

"Thank you," I tell her. "You want something to eat?"

Winter nods and I lead her into the kitchen, where we're both subjected to the boozy attention of my mother's two best friends, Marla and Cleo. She's known them since they were all in high school together, and while they're not the worst people in the world, they're too nosy for my taste.

"We hear you're not coming," Marla says to me in a singsong voice.

"Where's my mom?" I ask.

"Upstairs. She'll be down soon. She's getting her eyelashes glued on."

"He's not going?" Cleo echoes. "Why not?"

Marla waves a hand. "Oh, you know how Gus is. Angry and antisocial."

"That's me," I say. "Angry and antisocial."

She grins. "Just like your dad."

"You think?"

"I do." Marla sets her glass down to pull Winter into her arms. "But don't let it rub off on this one. She's too sweet for bad boys. Isn't that right, Winnie?"

36.

Just like your dad.

Ten minutes later they leave and I'm alone and I don't feel good about it. Not that I wanted to go but maybe I should've. Or maybe I should've wanted to.

Still standing in the kitchen, I grab for a glass, fill it with tap water, and gulp it down. Then I pour another. But something feels wrong. Really wrong. It's selfish and stupid and self-absorbed, but I don't think I can stay in this house right now. I don't think I can handle the fact that almost everyone I know is spending the night thinking about Danny.

The hardest part is knowing Lainey will be there. It's pathetic, but I still stalk her social media when I'm in one of my more self-pitying moods. Her post this afternoon was of an old photo of her and my brother, where Danny has his arms wrapped around her perfect waist, looking happier than I ever remember seeing him. For her part, Lainey's as perfect as she always is, brown eyes radiating warmth. The photo's caption was just a link to the club's dedication ceremony announcement, and I almost sent her a message when I saw it, but nothing I could think to say sounded right or said what I wanted her to know.

I miss you.

Don't go.

Be with me instead.

The glass slips from my hand to shatter on the tile floor.

"Fuck." Reaching for the broom, I drop to my knees and begin cleaning. I want to get out of here—I need to—but I don't want Winter to come home and cut herself. I end up using a whole roll of paper towels because the glass is a bitch to pick up. Glittering shards have scattered everywhere, and as I collect them, one by one, it's a struggle not to give in to the bloody promise of solace their sharpness offers. To drag them across my own skin.

It's actually a solace I gave in to a few times when I was younger. That is until some shitty kid in sixth-grade PE class saw my wounds while we were changing and told the teacher what I was doing. It's how I first got sent to therapy. A miserable experience: my mother took it upon herself to inform the therapist that my actions meant I was both emotionally needy and attention seeking because Danny and Darien had done similar things at my age.

When the kitchen is finally clean and free from temptation, I move fast, grabbing my swim stuff and leaving the house. Then I drive toward the Clayton Valley pool because it's the only place I can picture being that's not wholly intolerable.

When I arrive, it's earlier than my usual time and people are still there—the remains of a dwindling late-season cookout from the looks of it. The air reeks of charcoal and meat, and a cluster of preteen kids are splashing in the pool, spraying each other with water rifles.

I scan my key and walk inside. The air's thick with fluttering moths and velvety gloom. Dusk floats down, darkening the sky, and with my goggles in hand, I approach the kids in the pool to ask if they'll let me use a lane. But before I can reach them, I stop, startled.

There's a man on the pool deck. He's sitting right in front of me on a lounge chair, mere yards away. He's also cloaked in shadows, which is why I didn't see him before. But he must be someone's dad because he's got a beer in one hand, his phone close by, but nothing about him is relaxed. I observe him for a moment: how he scans the pool, his muscles tense, alert, never once easing in vigilance.

Never once noticing me.

My heart rolls over and dies and screw asking for a lane. I pull my goggles on, toss my towel down, and with a running start, I fling my body into the air, diving, stretching for the deep end. At the last moment, right before entering the water, I tuck my head and flail my limbs out, ensuring that my whole body hits the surface with a resounding smack and splash.

37

I loved Danny until the day I didn't. I loved him after he gave up on helping me learn to swim. I loved him when he actively tried to stop me from pursuing the same sport that he did—using mostly shame tactics and brute intimidation. Also rules. Danny had a lot of rules. For a while there, I couldn't speak to him if he didn't speak first. I couldn't eat near him. Or drink. Or play music. Or have friends over. Or even use the shared bathroom between our bedrooms without asking if he needed it before me.

Defying my brother's rules was always a gamble. Sometimes he didn't care and other times he'd scream. Or push me. Or worse, he'd lock himself in his room and refuse to come out, which meant getting yelled at by our mother for not being considerate of Danny's feelings. He was sensitive, she'd tell me. I *knew* that.

Yeah, I did, but over time it grew harder for me to care. Plus the older I got, the more I liked pushing Danny's buttons. I had nothing to lose and besides, I was good at it. It was the only thing I ever got credit for. If he was the hero, I was the villain, and it was a role I was born to play.

So I did.

This is also how I found my way back to swimming. First by joining the city rec league in eighth grade and later by making my high school team. I paid for everything I needed with money earned mowing lawns, walking dogs, and working on team fund-raisers. All my mother had to do was sign the waiver slips and get my medical clearance, which she did, if only in the hope that her lack of interest would demoralize me.

What she didn't count on was my stubborn streak. My ability to play the long game so long as it meant that someday, someway, I'd prove her wrong.

38

Jumping into the Clayton Valley pool the obnoxious way that I do, I'm able to scare off the kids with the water rifles, along with their solemn beer-drinking dad. Or maybe they were on the verge of leaving anyway—the sky's gone dark, the bugs are out. Regardless, I do what I always do: I swim.

After a quick warm-up, I chase perfection in the form of rigorous drills meant to build my muscles, my stamina, my technique. Once I'm done with those, I cycle through the drills again and again, pushing myself not to compromise on form. Or effort. Doing everything the right way's the only way to get better, and I'm meticulous in my focus. Then comes speed work. My main set's grueling, a tough rotation of maximum effort and minimal recovery. It's exhausting but I tell myself: just one more lap. And one more after that.

And after that one, too.

No matter how much I swim, it's not enough to erase the fact that it's still easier to drown. That I'm alone and unloved. But by the end, I've logged exactly 5,300 meters and when I crawl from the pool, the moon's out and the night is silent. I wrap my towel around my waist and sit my ass on a plastic chair. Everyone from the party earlier is gone and even though this is what I wanted, my loneliness comes alive. It's both claustrophobic and all-encompassing. It's in the night. The pool.

My skin.

Fuck Danny, I think.

Fuck everyone who worshipped the ground he walked on.

"Your instinct wasn't so killer, was it?" I call out.

Followed by: "I'm better than you. I'm going to prove that someday, I swear to God. No matter who tries to stop me."

More words pile up in my throat. A thickening traffic jam of anger and anguish and burning resentment. But before I can say more, my phone chirps from somewhere deep inside my swim bag. I bend down and go digging for it. Who could be texting me at ten o'clock on a Friday night? Danny's thing at the club is long over, so there's no point in yelling at me for not going. But when I find the phone, I'm stunned—it's Coach Marks.

His message reads: *Hey. You around?*

I type back: *What's up?*

He replies: *Think you'll be ready to swim for me next weekend?*

Part Two

39

I'm more than ready.

On the following Friday, we fly from Oakland to San Diego. There are six of us total—including Coach M—traveling to the upcoming meet taking place on the UC San Diego campus. Fitz and Vince act like they're bored because they've done this before, but for me and the other two new guys on the developmental roster, Caleb and Raheem, there's a palpable sense of anticipation. We know Coach M doesn't let anyone swim for the hell of it. He does it because he knows we can win.

Everyone responds to pressure in their own way. Caleb gets up to piss every five minutes, which means I have to get up, too, seeing as I'm in the aisle seat and he refuses to give up the window. In the center, between us, Raheem has serious diarrhea of the mouth; he won't stop talking—and not about swimming. He's been telling us about his girlfriend, Fiona, who he met online and as far as I can tell, has not met in person and may not even exist.

"But you've called her?" Caleb asks for the millionth time. He's got the same catfish suspicions as I do. "Like, you've heard her real voice?"

"Yeah," Raheem says. "I've heard her voice."

"And you've seen her?"

"Not in the flesh. But pictures, sure. Tons of them. All the time."

"What about FaceTime?"

"Her phone doesn't FaceTime."

"Snapchat?"

"Her mom won't let her."

"Fuck, dude." Caleb shakes his head sadly. "Do you even hear yourself?"

"You're just jealous."

"You're desperate."

They go back and forth like this, until I finally slide my earbuds in and turn my music up. Stress, in and of itself, is not a bad thing. Like right now, I feel good, excited, but even that kind of energy has to be handled in a way most beneficial to my endgame. At the moment, my body needs rest. So I'm not talking, not moving, not investing in the world around me. Case in point: I can still hear Caleb and Raheem bickering about fake girlfriends and who's gotten the closest to getting laid, but when Caleb taps me on the shoulder, laughing, to ask my opinion about something, I wave him off. And when he does it again, I get up and ask Fitz if he'll switch seats with me so that I can sit next to Coach Marks and not these idiots who're acting like we're on a booze cruise to Cabo.

"Seriously?" Fitz says, but finally acquiesces, which is the problem with trying to be a leader or role model. It puts you in the position of having to do the right thing.

"What's up?" Coach Marks asks when I'm settled.

"Tell me about the race," I say.

"Right now?"

"Why not?"

"There'll be time later. We have a team meeting at six tonight."

"But we have a whole plane ride now," I say.

It's kind of hard to argue with this fact, and he gives in, pulling his tray down and getting out his notebook to show me exactly what I'll be up against in the water. And who. Honestly, it doesn't sound like a lot of competition, other than Fitz and a guy from Santa Barbara who's been winning everything in the western states. His times don't intimidate me, though, so I don't get what the big deal is. Anyone can win a lot if they don't swim against high-quality swimmers. It doesn't make them special.

After explaining all that, Coach Marks launches into what he wants to see from me. It feels as if he's giving instructions to the jockey he's chosen to put on his best horse. Like he believes it'll be *his* brain controlling my body in the water and it's up to him to communicate his game plan to my brain in the most effective manner. I might as well have my earbuds in again for this part of the lecture. He's got the process all wrong, the way most coaches do. Us swimmers, we're more horse than jockey, so you can tell us whatever the hell you want but it won't matter. Come race day, everything that happens in the pool is up to us and only us.

One hundred percent.

40.

At the hotel I end up rooming with Fitz. That's fine with me—if I have to room with someone, it might as well be the guy who's done this before and won. At the least I won't be subjected to Raheem's late-night sexting with his imaginary girlfriend. Or Caleb's bladder issues and Vince's ego.

Fitz lets me choose the bed I want—the one by the window, naturally—and the first thing he does is take a shower. Airplanes are filthy, he tells me, and I'm sure he's right, but I don't know what a shower's going to be able to do about it this late in the game.

When he comes out, I'm in bed. Under the covers even.

"What the hell is this?" he barks.

"I'm sleeping."

"You're definitely not sleeping. Your eyes are open."

"That's because you're talking to me."

"It's not even six o'clock. And we've got a meeting in ten minutes."

"Fuck that."

"What?"

"I don't need to go to any meeting. Coach M went over everything on the plane."

Fitz glares. "You know, there are things we do for the greater good. It's called being part of a team."

"But we're not a team. Not in the water."

"What about the relay?"

"What do you mean?"

"You're swimming in one."

I groan. "Look, I'll do my part. I promise. Just leave me alone."

He pauses. "You serious?"

"Very."

"So you're just going to stay here and jack off and screw the rest of us?"

"Guess so," I say, although what I really plan on doing is resting. Sleep has been elusive lately, but tonight I'll need all I can get. However I can get it.

"Christ," Fitz mutters.

But he leaves.

41.

Once he's gone, I crash hard. Travel exhausts me in a way physical exertion never has, and the sleep I fall into is too deep for dreams but too good to last. I wake up gasping near midnight and in a panic. Everything's black. My pulse is racing, my ears are ringing, and for an instant I don't know where I am. Or why.

Then it comes to me.

You're in the Hyatt in San Diego.

Your first real meet is tomorrow.

Fitz snores like a monster from across the room. I get up to turn on the fan as a means to drown him out. Then I try earplugs but it's hopeless. I can't sleep. My body's twitchy. Unsettled. And for good reason: the process of preparing for a race doesn't just involve getting a lot of sleep the night before. There's also a reduction in training load in the week leading up to a meet. It's called tapering and the agitation it causes has its own name:

Taper madness.

I'm madder than most, I guess, because I need to get out of here. I need to do something. Swinging my legs to the floor, I fumble in the dark for clothing, then abandon the room with nothing but my phone and key. A strange migratory urge has taken over and I cruise the hotel corridors, fingers skimming along glossed wallpaper, down stair railings, and more.

In the lobby, I discover that not much is happening. A clerk dozes at the front desk and the hotel bar is in the process of shutting down. There's a pool on the property somewhere. I know this.

But it's no doubt long closed, and hopping the fence to dive in probably wouldn't turn out too well for me. My urges takes me elsewhere; I find an exit and leave.

Outside, beneath the whisper of the moon, the sidewalk has its way with me. I follow it out of the development, away from the row of sleeping hotels, sleeping restaurants, and the occasional gas station. My breath, my actions, feel reckless. This is who I am.

This is what I do.

The sidewalk grows cracked, weary, but it doesn't stop and neither do I. It leads me doggedly through intersection after intersection, and where it goes, I follow, follow, follow, until finally, at last, I can smell the ocean, feel its salt-sting burn, and I've made it. I start to run as my ears fill with the roar of the waves, the crash of the surf.

When I reach the beach, I kick off my shoes and grind my heels in the sand to let the earthiness take hold. Then I walk to the water's edge. It's agony, not being able to swim. Not being able to dive deep beneath the waves to soothe my rattled mind. But I'm here, I tell myself. I'm alive. I don't need to offer myself up to the ocean in an act of sacrifice or suffering.

It's enough to know I can.

42.

Fitz is awake when I return to the room at daybreak with salt in my hair, salt on my skin. He doesn't ask where I've been, and I don't offer. Instead I head for the shower. For more solitude.

"We're meeting for breakfast in thirty minutes," he says.

"Okay."

"You coming?"

Stepping out of the bathroom while the water heats, I reach for my gear bag and pull it open to double, triple check that I've got everything I need. "Yeah. I'll be there."

~~~~~~~~~~

Fitz doesn't wait for me and I head down for breakfast on my own. I take the elevator this time and find that the lobby's been transformed. No longer desolate, the place is packed with scores of swimmers, all bunched together by team, by age.

It's a lot to take in.

I find Coach Marks and the other guys waiting outside the dining room. I'm not late or anything, so I don't bother apologizing, even though I'm the last one to show up. The bleary expressions on Raheem's and Caleb's faces hint that their nights were as restless as my own. Vince, however, appears unfazed and Fitz is screwing around on his phone. Before we go in to eat, Coach M asks if we can talk.

"Sure," I say. "What's up?"

"What happened to you last night?"

"When?"

"When you missed our meeting."

"I was sleeping."

"Before dinner?"

"I was beat."

"What'd you do when you woke up?" he asks.

"How do you know I woke up?"

"You look like shit."

"I took a walk," I say.

"At night?"

"Yeah."

"By yourself?"

"That's right."

His brow wrinkles and I get the feeling he wants to ask more about what I was doing. But what he says is, "You miss another meeting, you don't swim for me. Got it?"

I nod but say nothing because it's not really a question. Luck's with me, though, and Coach Marks seems satisfied and we move on to the breakfast portion of the morning. Stepping into the hotel buffet is a surreal experience. This isn't like the high school meets I've been to. For those we always stayed in crappy motels—four to a room—and ate Pop-Tarts and hard-boiled eggs that we'd stored overnight in the mini fridges. In contrast, this place has white tablecloths and hot food, and the ratio of swimmers to coaches is a lot smaller than I'm used to. High school meets are loud, raucous, and buzzing with frat-house hormones. You always get the feeling the coaches are on the verge of losing control and that half the kids are just going through the motions so they can try to get laid in the hot tub later.

The mood here is more subdued. *Focused* might be a better word, but the point is that it's quiet. Maybe it's a social cue taken from the tablecloths. I don't know, really, but I start to feel sick while I'm picking out what I want to eat because people are watching me and I know I'm taking too long.

I'm on the verge of panicking when Coach Marks comes up behind me and asks what I'm waiting for. His tone is lighthearted—I've been forgiven—so I mumble something about too many choices.

"Get the oatmeal," he says. "Some juice, yogurt, a bagel with cream cheese, and the eggs."

"Is that all?" I ask.

"You'll need it."

He's right, of course, and I pile my tray with everything he says. Then I join the others. We eat fast, and I get down what I can while Coach Marks goes over the call times for our events. It'll be more than two hours before I'm in the water, but this includes us getting our shit together, riding the shuttle over to the swim complex at the university, checking into the facility, changing, and warming up.

Two hours is nothing.

From here on out, my actions are preemptive. Proactive. I don't wait for Raheem to irritate me or for Fitz to chew gum or for me to get annoyed by overhearing someone else's bullshit on the shuttle. The minute we leave the hotel and head for the meet, I slip in my earbuds and tune the fuck out.

It's game time.

43

The buildup's endless. We reach the UCSD aquatic facility, where we still have to make our way through registration. The line's long, slow, but it's the only way to gain access to the changing rooms and pools, and it's hard not to stare at the streams of people coming in to watch the meet. It'll be *packed*. But I force myself to focus on the mundane. No matter how big the venue, all swim meets involve the same steps. You get in. Change. Warm up. Swim.

That's it, really.

Finally, we're through. Credentials in hand, we enter the venue by way of a large rec center and follow directions to the West Pool. Winding our way through the building, I take note of the changing rooms, a weight room, and dedicated space for personal training and physical therapy. It's impressive. Before we step outside, Coach Marks taps me on the shoulder and asks if I'd be willing to "have a chat" with someone whose name I don't recognize.

"Me?" I say, looking around.

He nods.

"Chat with who?"

He waves to Fitz, who shuffles off with the other guys, then motions for me to follow. I do and we head toward an open door adjacent to the restrooms. But I'm confused. This is clearly a planned detour. Is this about the meeting I missed? Have I done something else wrong?

"—not a big deal in the least," Coach Marks is telling me. "They just want to get to know you. Smile and nod. Be polite.

That's it. You don't need to get into anything complicated."

"Wait, *what*?" My head feels muddled. I don't know how I missed what he was saying. It's the noise, I guess. The crowd.

"In here." We walk through the open door and up a flight of stairs that opens into a media room of some sort. It's a wide space set over the swim complex and it's got this huge glass viewing window that's angled over each of the aquatic center's twin pools. West is where we'll be swimming and East is hosting the diving competition. There are rows of tables filled with laptops, cameras, and what I assume are sports journalists. A tall woman in a black suit walks over to us.

"Colin," she says briskly. "Thanks for coming."

"My pleasure," Coach Marks says.

The woman turns to me, extends her hand. "I'm Renee Matheson. I'm with *Swimming World*."

"I'm Gus Bennett."

"I know who you are," she says. "Would it be all right if I asked you a few questions?

"About what?"

She smiles. "Nothing too difficult, I hope."

I glance at Coach Marks, then nod. "Yeah. Okay, sure."

"First of all, how old are you?"

"Sixteen. I'll be seventeen next month."

"And what are you hoping to do here today?"

"Win?"

The woman laughs. "Glad to hear it."

"Thank you," I say.

"It'd be quite a surprise, though, wouldn't it? Winning?"

"Why's that?"

"Well, I've seen your times," she says.

My spine stiffens. "Then you haven't seen anything."

"Well, I'm a fan of your confidence."

"Okay."

She pauses, turning serious. "You know, I'm sorry about your brother. I had the pleasure of meeting him a few times. He was a great swimmer."

"I guess," I say.

"Well, what do you think Danny would tell you if he were here?"

"What would he *tell* me?"

"Yeah, what would his mind-set be coming into a situation like this?"

"How the hell should I know? I'm not Danny."

"I just mean—"

Coach Marks steps in, pulls me back. "We have to get him down to the pool now, Renee. Thank you so much for your time. We can talk later. I'll give you a call."

The woman nods. "I'd like that. Thanks for setting this up, Colin."

"Sure thing."

"Good luck today." She hands me her card before walking away.

44.

"You all right?" Coach M asks as we walk down the ramp to the lower level.

I don't answer. I don't know how I am, and I didn't like what just happened.

Not at all.

"I should've warned you she'd ask about Danny. I'm sorry."

I shake my head. "I should've expected it. I mean, everyone's going to ask me about him, won't they? It's the only reason they'd want to talk to me in the first place."

"For now, yes."

"You think that'll change?"

"If you win," he says. "Even then, not for a while."

Well, I appreciate the honesty. We keep walking, and when I look at him next, Coach Marks has this small smile on his face. A sly one, which is a rarity for him as far as I know.

"What's so funny?" I ask.

His smile grows wider. "You want to know what Danny would've told you if he were here?"

"What?"

"Not a fucking thing."

This is both true and funny and I want to laugh, if only to break the tension, to bond, to feel a little fucking human. But I *can't*. It's my nerves, I guess. Or that interview.

I look over my shoulder.

"Hey, hey, Gus—it's okay," Coach Marks tells me.

"What?" I whip my head back around to stare at him.

"However it is you're feeling right now. If this is hard for you, then that's okay. Just let it be what it is."

I nod. Quickly. "Thank you."

Then: "I'm totally fine."

"I know you are," he says.

45.

Out on the pool deck, it's utter mayhem. The surrounding bleachers are packed with spectators, leaving teams to set up their rest areas on the cement and grass. Coach Marks points to where Fitz has staked out a spot for us, and it's basically a miracle that we find them. There's scarcely room to move, much less relax. There's also no rhyme or reason to our location; it simply exists in a sea of banners and pop-ups and folding chairs and snack tables and wet towels and swimmers who are sprawled all over the place eating food, studying textbooks, playing games on their phones, or sleeping. Music pours from about a million different speakers, a wild cacophony, and it's impressive that anyone can hear or see anything that's happening in the actual pool at all.

I take a seat in a chair and face the pool. People like to complain about how long swim meets are—that you wait around all day to get in the water for a total of thirty seconds. And while this is technically true, every sport has its own rhythm and rules. Besides, *waiting* isn't an accurate word for what happens at a meet. Waiting is passive, something people do only when they've accepted that their fate is in the hands of others.

It's safe to say that no one here is passive or running out the clock until they get to swim. All of us are engaged in some sort of mental preparation. You have to be at this level. What I personally focus on is maintaining a high level of intensity, and I do this by reminding myself how I got here. How I'm not like the other athletes. I didn't grow up on swim meets and praise and weeknights spent racing against the guys and hoping my coach would notice me. Instead, for a long time, for years, I simply watched my brother. It was all I *could* do, seeing as the closest I ever got to a pool was watching Danny practice and compete. So I watched everything he did, and despite my growing resentment toward him, it was thrilling. He deserved the limelight. Absolutely. He was good. Better than good.

He was the best.

It wasn't until later that the bitterness really seeped in, urging me to seek out my own glory. Even then, it wasn't Danny that I was mad at so much as myself. And the reason for this was that Darien had moved back home. This was the year I turned twelve and my sister was using then—she'd overdosed twice—and our mother tried desperately to get her into rehab. It didn't work. Addiction being what it is, Darien toyed with her, always wavering between contrition and total self-destruction.

She was also destructive in other ways. Like the time she and Danny took it upon themselves to tell me the truth about my father's death and let me know I was the one responsible for it. Partially, at least. All I'd known prior was that my father had died in a car crash before I was born. But the real story was more complicated, Darien said with a smile. The real story was that when our mother was seven months pregnant with me, I stopped moving inside her.

She totally panicked, Darien said, but did everything her pregnancy books recommended—drank orange juice, played loud music, and jabbed her swollen belly in an effort to wake me up. But nothing worked, and when she got her ob-gyn on the phone, she was told in no uncertain terms to get to the ER *now*. At this point, our mother went into crisis mode. She dumped Darien and Danny at a neighbor's house, called my father's work, where she left a frantic message about where she was going and why, and bolted for the hospital.

My father, who worked in construction, was at a jobsite down in Alamo at the time. The way Darien told it, when he got the message, he dropped the phone and sprinted for his truck, hopping onto the northbound highway and heading straight for the hospital. That's the part of the story that kills me. The fact that my mother never asked him to come, but that he did anyway.

It was late afternoon. Rush-hour traffic on the interstate was sucky and I'll always wonder if my father grew impatient. If he contemplated jerking the wheel, pulling onto the shoulder, and just hitting the gas, willing to take the heat from the cops if he got pulled over. But he didn't get that chance. Less than five minutes after hearing my mother's voice for the very last time, my father was rear-ended by a distracted big-rig driver as he sat at a complete stop on a six-lane highway.

This meant that while my mother was in the ER, lying on an exam table for an ultrasound in which she finally watched me stretch and move inside her, after waking up on my own damn time, first responders twenty miles away were using the Jaws of Life to free my father from his crushed vehicle. A hopeless exercise: he'd died on impact, his life snuffed out for good as my mother broke down in that exam room, sobbing with relief and thanking God that her prayers had been answered.

My siblings told me this story on a night when the three of us were huddled in the backyard around a firepit. Around me sparks and flame leapt toward the sky, and I don't remember where our mother was, only that I felt scared and guilty and also filled with the most overwhelming sense of understanding.

Of course, I thought.

Of course.

I still don't know if they were right to tell me the way that they did. And I still don't know if they were trying to inflict pain or save me from it. But in the end, it explained everything, didn't it? Why my mother hated me.

Why Danny did, too.

Later, I crawled into bed in my room on the second floor. An open skylight looked out at the stars—a whole summer sky filled with them. Wondrous. Dazzling.

"I'm sorry," I whispered. "I'm so, so sorry."

46

"Medley relay team on deck," Coach M barks, as if we didn't hear the announcer say the exact same thing thirty seconds ago. He's excited for us, though. I can hear it in his voice, see the gleam in his eye. He lives for this.

Well, so do I.

I shake myself out of my bad memories, my bad mood. This is the reason I race, after all. The four of us—Caleb, Raheem, Fitz, and me—shuffle toward the pool in a bunch, each of us adjusting our goggles, our suits, making sure our muscles stay loose. Fitz and I are the only two who haven't gotten in the water yet this morning. Raheem finished second in his IM heat, which means he'll move on to the finals later, and Caleb was third in his, which means he won't. For the relay, there're only five other teams entered in the event, so there's no need for qualifying heats.

It's one and done.

We line up in order of our legs. I'm last—the anchor—swimming freestyle, while Raheem will kick us off with the backstroke. That leaves Caleb to do breast and Fitz fly. Coach Marks gathers us around him for last-minute instructions, which I barely make note of because all I want is for the other guys to swim their goddamn asses off. I'll win it for them from there.

Standing behind the block in those few seconds of calm before the race begins, I glance out at the crowd, my gaze moving up toward the media box where all those cameras are lined up in anticipation of capturing greatness. I roll my neck and hope to God that Renee Matheson's watching.

That she sees what I can do.

The horn blows and the race does, too. Raheem flails with a bad start from the wall, swiftly falling behind, and Caleb's no match for his competition. He gives up, from what I can tell, and even though Fitz's leg is strong—all power and rhythm—there's only so much he can do. By the time my leg starts, we're more than half a pool length behind. I make up what I can but we end up third overall. So much for showing what I can do. So much for anything.

Fitz pulls me from the pool. "Nice finish."

"Who the fuck cares?" I snap.

He rolls his eyes and I sulk inwardly, alight with resentment. As a kid, I can remember watching the Cowboys miss a field goal after Tony Romo botched the snap and John Madden saying he hated it when coaches left their quarterbacks in on fourth down. If they were there, it was only because their previous play had failed, and that was where their mind would be. Madden's point was that you don't put someone who's pissed in a position where you need them to go out and score on the very next play. This is all a long way of saying I don't get why Coach M would have me swim in that relay knowing we didn't have a shot. Now my mind's fixated on a loss in a race I didn't even want to swim, and my better races are still to come.

No one talks to me after the relay. Especially not Caleb and Raheem. Instead they sit together and glower at me and let me tell you, there are two types of athletes in this world: the ones who let themselves get sucked into petty drama and ones who know how to move the fuck on.

Rally, I tell myself.

Optics are everything.

To this end, I drop my head, let my shoulders droop, and make my way over to where Coach M is sitting.

"Hey, would you tell me something?" I ask.

"What's that?"

"I know what Danny would've said to me before a race. But what did you use to say to him?"

Coach Marks blinks in surprise, turning to look up at me, and I wish I resembled my brother more than I already do. He took after our mother, with her high cheekbones and burnished skin. My overall build is similar, but my features are sharper, more angled and I have our father's darker eyes, darker everything.

"You really want to know?" he says.

I nod.

"Why?"

"Not sure."

"Well, sit down," he says, and there's real tenderness to his tone. Like he's been waiting for this moment, the chance to nurture and guide me, or maybe just the chance to talk about his favorite swimmer. But I sit and nod and say "Uh-huh" whenever he pauses in the story he's telling me. It's some anecdote about Danny and his anxiety, which followed him well into adolescence, even as he outgrew a lot of his childhood fears. Doctors wrote him numerous prescriptions to manage it over the years, although he was loath to take them for fear of testing positive for something unexpected. Obviously there's *another* reason I knew about the pills Danny was given and why he didn't take them, but that's not something I like to think about.

Coach Marks keeps talking to me in that slow, soothing voice of his. Now he's recounting the details of some grounding exercise Danny liked to do. It sounds real out-there, that kind of *"feel your feet connected to the earth and plant your roots deep beneath you"* type of thing. I'm pretty sure Danny would've laughed in my face if I ever suggested something like this. But instead of laughing, I stay seated right beside Coach M and try to act the way Danny might've, because I want people to see us together and think of him.

I want them to believe I'm supposed to be here.

My 200 m heat's called over the loudspeaker, and Coach Marks reaches to pat my shoulder while giving me one last useless pep talk ("Don't go out too fast!" "Make your turns count!"). Then it's time. I stand and gaze out at the crowd, and I know the damage has been repaired. Not between me and Caleb or Raheem. But between me and *them*. Everyone who's watching. Everyone whose energy and passion I plan to exploit.

Squaring my shoulders, I hold my head high as I walk to my lane. The deck's wet, cold beneath my feet. In movies, whenever there's a big race or competition, the crowd goes silent at the start, their collective breath bated. But in reality, there's always noise and movement. There's no such thing as silence. Or calm.

Only vision.

47

I step up on the block with a shimmer of disconnect. Of imbalance.

Breathe, I remind myself, and I take a page from Danny's play-book by focusing on the way my heels press down against the gritty surface beneath me. It may be holding me up, but at least I'm the one on top. I don't bother looking at the other racers. That's not energy I'm willing to expend today. Instead I bend at the waist, adjust my goggles, and set my sights on the surface below.

It's electric right now. The water is charged. Alive.

I lift my head.

The horn blows and I'm gone.

48.

Everything's faster in a race. Too fast, almost, but my entry's sharp, clean, followed by the wild rush and squeeze of cold-struck lungs. Any hint of panic and this is when you fail, when the liquid underworld sucks you in and pulls you under and has its way with you. It's all over then, and there's nothing you can do because the start doesn't happen when you hit the water but in all the times you've hit it before.

Bubbles clear. The black lane lines come into view and I surge forward with full-body force. There are no limbs down here. No mind separate from the body. There's only execution and form. Swimming or stillness. My whip-crack dolphin kick propels me along the cool belly of the pool until the laws of physics shove me to the surface and I corkscrew my way into my stroke.

My pace is strong, even, pure torque and pull, and I surrender to the near-perfect rhythm of my ability. This is the speed I've practiced and the power I've mastered. It's only when I'm confident in what my muscles, my blood, and my breath tell me that I push for more. Then more again. It holds; there's no slipping in my timing, my strength—I want this. I want it all.

I can't tell where anyone else is, but it doesn't matter. The path to victory is the one I fight for. I push my speed again, chewing through the water, and after the first turn, I know I've got this. It's *in* me. I take the second turn clean and throw myself into the final hundred.

The crowd cheers, a wild, throaty roar, and something's happening. This race is close or someone's making a last-minute break.

My body responds before my brain can tell it what to do but I rise to the call, imploring every part of myself to *Push, push, you stupid bastard. You're nothing if you give up now. Do it, you asshole.*

The pain sets in. My lungs burn, my arms tire beneath the drag of the water, but the last fifty's where the work goes. Not the day's effort, what I've done in this pool—but the countless laps, the stolen hours at night, the years of self-loathing and the lifetime of guilt. This is what it's been for. This is when it matters. And so I fight and I keep on fighting. There's no fade in my homestretch. No weakness in my attack. Only a full-throttle sprint for the end.

First my hand hits the wall, then my head, knocking my goggles askew and ringing my ears. The crowd continues to roar but why? I see nothing but foam. Chlorine burns my eyes, water rushes up my nostrils, down my throat, but I whip around to look at the scoreboard. The letters, the numbers, defy me, and I can't tell for sure how I've done until Coach Marks comes, grabs me by the arm.

"Did I win?" I gasp. "Did I make the final?"

He laughs. "You did more than that."

"What do you mean?"

"Apparently, you just set a pool record."

49.

It's all gravy from there. I beat out Fitz to take first in the finals. I beat my earlier time, too, and no, I don't grandstand up there at the awards ceremony. But I could. I've earned it.

I've earned real attention, too, although I know this is fleeting. Renee Matheson tells Coach Marks they'll definitely be running a feature on me in the next issue. It's great news, obviously, although any swimmer can have a good day, a good race, some earthly moment of godliness. It's what I'll do at the next meet and the next and the one after that that will define who I'll become and how I'll be talked about. But the seeds of interest have been planted. I just need to keep winning from here on out.

Fitz isn't happy with me after the meet. I don't blame him. I wouldn't be happy with me, either. He doesn't say any of this, but I get the feeling he expects me to thank him when we're alone again, back in the hotel together after our team dinner out at some shitty chain restaurant. Or at least acknowledge his leadership, the kindness he's shown me since I joined the team.

I don't, though. I'm too tired.

I fall into bed.

And sleep.

50.

The flight out of San Diego is an early one. I oversleep my alarm and have to scramble to get ready, meaning I'm the last one to the lobby. Once we're in the sky, though, all the other guys crash. Even Coach Marks, who has his tablet out and is pretending to read, nods off, a slight line of drool running from the corner of his mouth. It's the hum of the engines, I suppose, the dimming of the lights.

I resist returning to my dreams. Too much is spinning through my mind. Too many things I need to do. My future will require doubling down on my efforts and even though it's what I wanted, something feels wrong. Misguided. It's hard to explain, but almost by instinct I push away thoughts of how I stood at the edge of the ocean two nights ago. How I craved something I couldn't find. I want to believe I found it at the meet yesterday. And to that end, I spend the next sixty minutes staring out the window at the sunrise while mentally reliving my best race in the hope that it'll clear my head. Brighten my mood.

But it doesn't.

The descent into Oakland begins with a steep dip and roll that leaves me clammy. Sitting up straight, I lean forward to glance around the cabin only to find that everyone's asleep. Hungover, maybe. Or dead. There's another a jolt, a sharp one, and I feel my breakfast rising in my throat. *Fuck.* I squeeze my eyes shut, grip the armrest, and tell myself planes are supposed to move with the wind, not resist it.

I stay like this until the plane touches down and the lights come on and everything and everyone around comes to life again. Vince pulls his phone out and turns it on before looking over at me.

"You okay?" he asks.

Am I?

"Yeah," I say.

51

It's a relief to be off the plane and outside, but my stomach remains unsettled because my mom doesn't show up at baggage claim. Or anywhere. She also doesn't answer when I text asking where the hell she is, so when Coach Marks offers me a ride, I have no choice but to accept.

"Thanks," I say.

"No problem."

"So where do you live?" I ask once we've boarded the shuttle that will take us to long-term parking.

"Alamo."

"You drive all the way from Alamo to Lafayette? Every day?"

"Indeed."

"How's the traffic?"

"It's fine."

"Why don't you move closer?"

"I don't want to be closer."

Fair enough. Fifteen minutes later, we're in his Lexus, turning onto the highway. I press my head into the seat back and squint out at blue sky, but the air looks smoggy. Unclean. My stomach cramps and I flip on the air-conditioning. Tap my fingers against the door handle.

"How're your muscles this morning?" Coach M slips a Tic Tac into his mouth. Offers me one, which I decline. "You sore?"

"Not really."

"You should be."

"Are we swimming tonight?" I ask. "Is there practice?"

"Are you kidding me?"

"Well, then what's next? What's the plan? When's the next race?"

"Recovery comes next."

"What?"

"We go home and sleep, Gus. You need to rest."

"No, no, no. I don't want to sleep. I don't want to fucking go home, either. I want to *do* something."

Right then his phone chirps and Coach Marks answers it, shoving a Bluetooth speaker in his ear. I don't know who it is he's talking to, but his side of the conversation is boring. I catch a couple snips of "Can you get a second opinion?" and "I can swing by later but make sure she's drinking water," which makes me think of either an ill family member or an ailing pet. I tune out what I can and sink lower into my seat.

He hangs up as we cruise into Lafayette and head for Lynnwood Court. I don't have to give him directions. He knows where I live.

"Sorry about that." He nods at the phone.

"It's fine."

We pull up to the house and my mother's car is right there in the driveway. She's definitely home and she definitely didn't care enough to come and get me or even to tell me she wouldn't. Coach Marks pulls up in front of the house and sets the brake, lets the engine idle. I sit there for a moment, but she doesn't come running out to greet me.

"Everything going all right at home?" Coach M asks.

"How would I know?"

"Your mom's an intense person. She's . . ."

I turn to look at him. "She's what?"

"She's very sad."

I roll my eyes, grab my bag. "Yeah, well, she should be."

"What's that supposed to mean?"

"It means everything in her life's a mess right now. That's not something she's equipped to deal with. It's pathetic."

"That's it?"

"Should there be more?"

"You tell me," he says, and I know there's something deeper he's asking for, something darker. But there are answers he doesn't need to know and ones I don't need to say.

"Thanks for the ride." I reach for the door.

He lifts his hand in farewell. "No problem."

~~~~~~~~~~~~~~~~

When he's driven away, out of sight, I scramble to where the Mink's parked at the end of the cul-de-sac. Unlocking the passenger-side door, I slide in and open the glove compartment. It takes a minute of digging through the trash my brother stuffed in here, but I find what I'm looking for.

It's the envelope. Thick, creamy, and sealed. And sure enough, the address written on the front is in the city of Alamo.

52.

After San Diego, school starts to fade into the background, a white-noise hum. This is a relief, even though I try to keep my grades up. It's just hard to get myself there every day. There are too many people. Too many distractions. I'm not interested in school, in general, although in econ we learn something that catches my attention. It's called black swan theory—the name given to phenomena that are completely unexpected but have a huge impact on the world. Like a dinosaur-killing meteor. Or a devastating plague. Or a reality-show host winning the highest office in the land.

According to this theory, the events themselves aren't notable so much as the way we respond to them. In the aftermath of a black swan event, it seems that human nature compels us to tell every single person who will listen why whatever it is that just happened *makes fucking total sense*. Despite the fact that no one saw it coming. Or because no one saw it coming. I guess the deeper point has less to do with how well we do or don't understand the world with any amount of certainty than with the bare truth that none of us has any idea how to sit with uncertainty.

I'm sure there's more to it than that, like the way we use lies to cover for failure. But what I took away from the whole discussion is that swimming is kind of a black swan sport. It relies so heavily on tradition. On what came before. There are programs and coaches and legacies that consistently churn out champion after champion after champion. You'd think this achievement would be worth something—*everything*—and yet nothing gets people on their feet and cheering more than the swimmer who comes out of nowhere.

The one they never saw coming.

This is me in the wake of the *Swimming World* spotlight, which gets printed in their October issue and attracts a lot of attention. Not only am I Danny Bennett's little brother—I'm utterly unheard of. I may as well have jumped in the pool for the first time this year for all anyone on the national level knows. My high school times were good but not *that* good, which only adds to the mystery of how I did what I did in San Diego, and my success is chalked up to:

Genes

Grief

Reincarnation

Not necessarily in that order. But no matter the cause, my story makes people want to keep watching me, which is perfect because the other thing that happens in the wake of the *Swimming World* spotlight is that I keep winning. Better still, I'm getting faster, closing in on my brother's best times. Closing in on destiny.

But I don't stop and bask in these accolades. I know better. It's when shit's clicking that you have to push harder. Get angrier. Be more willing to suffer.

I tell the team this, every chance I get. They don't want to hear it, but that doesn't mean I don't try. A rising tide lifts all ships or whatever and I'd sure as hell like to be lifted a little bit every now and then. And I mean, they sort of owe me, don't they?

"What the fuck are you going on about now?" This is Raheem, after I bring up the team's lack of drive after practice one day.

"I'm talking about really competing. Getting serious about what we're doing here."

"You don't think we're serious?" Vince gives me a long look.

"Not really. This whole club is kind of unmotivated."

"What're you doing here, then? *You* came to *us*, remember?"

I throw my hands in the air. "I guess I thought you'd be tougher than nine workouts a week."

"Oh, are you a coach now?"

"You know the junior national team is doing twelve pool work-outs a week. That's not including dry-land training. Look, I've been telling Coach M. Over and over. But it's not enough. If we all—"

"So go swim for the junior national team," someone says from behind me. I turn around but can't tell which of them said it.

"I would if I could," I say.

"Really?" Vince gives me a withering glare. "Well, I don't know about you, but I'm pretty happy right where I am."

"Me too," echoes Raheem.

"Fuck happy," I tell them. "Is that really what you're here for? That's all you want out of this?"

"You think we want to be like you and walk around pissed off all the time?"

"You should. If it gets you what you want."

Raheem stares at me. "Your brother could've used a little happiness in his life, don't you think?"

"No, I don't," I snarl. "He didn't need happiness. He needed to be a better goddamn swimmer."

Vince shakes his head. "I think you're sick, too, man. I mean that. You need help."

"At least I fucking win."

"Yeah, Gus," he says with a sigh. "At least you fucking win."

53.

Along with the magazine article, October brings a different form of salvation: my mother's absence from the house. I can't say I don't love this. This time of year is a blessed mix of wedding and crush season up in the wine country, meaning she's booked solid with photography jobs through the end of the month. She can't get out of them, either. Some of these events were reserved more than a year ago and my mom's partner can't do it all herself. Not even with the assistant she's brought in.

This is a good thing, for a lot of reasons: my mother paying the bills being the biggest one, followed by her staying out of my business. But even I know it's not healthy for her or Winter to stay locked up in this house all the time. So I breathe a sigh of relief when she enrolls Winter in a preschool during the week. I also end up watching her sometimes, although I try to discourage this. It's not that I don't like my niece—I do—but being with her has a way of making me so *sad*.

"What did we do?" I whisper to her on those late evenings when we watch television together in the living room. She sits pressed tight against me, like she wants us to stay attached. Like she wants to ensure I'll never leave. As it gets late and she gets tired, she does this thing where she shoves her thumb in her mouth and wraps the rest of her hand inside this sorry scrap of a blanket square she showed up with. It must smell like her mother—or else she imagines it does—because her head droops and her breathing slows, like a Mack truck settling into a gentle snore. Once she's all the way out, I don't take her upstairs, where her bedroom is. Instead I lay her on the couch, pull a blanket over her, and whisper again, "What did we ever do to deserve this?"

Winter never answers, and this is fine. Obviously, I know what I did to deserve my fate, and I know I'm projecting my own unhappiness onto her. I don't *want* Winter to feel the way that I do. But if she does, I tell myself, at least she'll know she's not alone.

At least I will, too.

~~~~~~~~~~

"What's this?" A few days later, my mother finds the *Swimming World* profile of me and dangles it in front of my face the moment I walk in the door after practice.

"What does it look like?" I push past her and collapse onto the couch in the living room. My sense of bleakness has been intensifying of late, coupled with a desire to stop moving because there's no meaning in movement when we'll all be dead someday anyway. I've been upping my training to compensate for what feels like laziness.

"Don't be a smartass," my mother says. "This is a really big deal."

"I know."

She pulls the magazine in front of her and stares down at the tiny photograph they printed of me. I'm standing in between Coach Marks and Fitz, and the look on my face is one of intense concentration. "I had no idea you were this serious."

"You could've asked."

"When's your next meet?"

"We're going to Portland in two weeks," I say.

"The Speedo Invitational?" She perks up. "You know, I swam in that way back when."

"I didn't know that."

"Hold on." She scoots out of the room and returns with a framed photograph of herself from years ago. She's standing on a podium in this giant swim jacket, holding a trophy. All sun-kissed and shining, she's practically glowing, and the look in her eyes says the world is hers for the taking.

"I was seventeen that year," she says. "Took first in the hundred-meter and two-hundred-meter backstroke. Second in IM. It's a big deal, getting to go up there. Trust me."

I'm the big deal is what I want to say. Instead I shrug.

My mother lingers. "What's Colin saying about your chances?"

"Who?"

"Your coach."

"Oh." I touch my temple. I knew that. "He thinks my chances are fine. He wouldn't send me if he didn't."

"God, they loved Danny in Portland."

"Why?" I ask.

She's startled by this question. "What do you mean? Everyone loved him."

I roll my eyes. "I didn't."

"Don't say that."

"Well, what did people love about him? What made him different from anyone else?"

This flicker of reverie comes over her, a bright flash of bliss. You can always spot it—the color rising in her cheeks when she's thinking about Danny in some context other than his death. "He just had this way of making people feel special when they were around him. I don't really know how to describe it."

"Sounds like a cult leader," I mutter.

"Not at all. Danny was too independent for that. It was more like he could make you feel lucky to be close to him."

"Is that how he made you feel?" I venture.

She smiles. "Sure. Sometimes."

"How do I make you feel?"

My mother looks down at me, her reverie broken, and she's frowning again. "What kind of question is that?"

"Just what I said."

"I don't know. You're different. More serious."

"Different in that you don't feel lucky to have me around?" I ask.

"I didn't say that."

"You kind of did."

Her eyes narrow. "Don't put words in my mouth, Gus. You always do this. It's like a fucking trap being with you."

"I'm not doing *anything*. I asked a question. I just want to understand *why*."

"Why what?" she says.

"Never mind. God."

She pulls the photograph of herself toward her body. Holds it close and out of my view. "Well, if you want me to be honest, that article that woman wrote. It sort of made you sound a little . . ."

"A little what?" I ask.

"Cold," she tells me.

54.

My mother's right about one thing: Portland *is* a big race. Fitz and I are the only guys from our team going, and when I look up who else is registered it's clear every top junior in the country is flying in to attend the three-day meet. It's one of the few events this fall that counts as a qualifier for the junior national team, although their selection process is a little more complicated—aka subjective—than it is for the national team.

Regardless, I don't have my sights set on the junior team. I want the real deal, but Portland still holds value for me. A good showing against the elite juniors will push me up in the rankings and make me eligible for my first nonjunior event in Vancouver in early December.

The path for someone my age making it to the national team and the Olympics isn't an easily laid-out one, because it's not supposed to happen. Not for guys anyway, who tend to mature later. But it is possible in a black swan sort of way, and I have no problem asserting myself as the guy to beat all odds.

"You're sure I should be swimming in all four events?" I ask Coach Marks as the Portland meet approaches. Even without a relay, he's got me entered in the 200 m free and 400 m free, as well as both distances in the IM. "You don't think I should focus on the freestyle? That's my best stroke."

"What do you want to do?" he counters. We're standing out on the pool deck after evening practice. It's cool October weather, a quiet night at the club. A pair of thirteen-year-old twins are warming up for a late clinic with Coach M while their parents watch from the bleachers, and this may not be the optimal time to be discussing something so significant. But it's the time I have.

"I want to do the *right* thing," I say. "I want to do what's best for me."

"So do I."

I wrap the towel around my waist tighter. "Well, you're the coach. You're supposed to know what that is."

"But I don't."

Is this a joke? "Why the fuck not?"

"I don't know you well enough to know what's right for you."

"How can you not *know* me?"

Coach Marks tilts his head. "We only met four months ago."

I fume. "So you took me on—knowing full well what my goal is—and now you have no clue how to get me there?"

"Is that really how you see it?" he asks.

"Absolutely."

"I'm sorry to hear that."

"That's all you have to say? That you're sorry? I pay your fucking *salary*!" I don't mean to raise my voice, but it happens and the twins and the parents are all looking at us, their eyes wide and worried, like a herd of spooked deer.

Coach Marks folds his arms. "I don't think you want to hear the rest of what I have to say."

God, I hate this. "I just want to *win*."

"I know."

"Then that's what matters. Not anything else. You don't need to know me any better than that to do your goddamn *job*."

"Go home, Gus," he sighs. "This isn't your time right now. I'll see you in the morning."

55

Yeah, well, fuck Coach Marks and fuck my mom because you know what? I go to Portland, swim in all four races, and I dominate.

Everything.

56.

I know the drill this time. I play it humble up there on the award podium, smiling, waving, and limiting myself to one-word answers when people yell questions at me like:

How did you do it?

Or:

What did your brother teach you?

And, my personal favorite:

Are you doing this for him?

All the while, Coach Marks doesn't leave my side. No doubt this is for his benefit more than mine, but I don't blame him. What happens in the water's up for grabs, but there's a whole script to winning and it's best not to deviate from it.

It's a script I couldn't help but glean from Danny. He really had the role down and he basked in it. I'll give him that. He was the guy who'd stay and answer every goddamn question, even if the person asking it was a kid from some local paper. In that way, Danny really did make people feel special. Like they were lucky to know him. But I knew him better and there wasn't an action he took or a kindness he faked that wasn't done solely for his own benefit.

I feel like this is what most people won't acknowledge about the heroes they choose to worship. They know they're being used, and they know their adoration is indulged for advancement or validation. In return they ask only that their heroes suffer for their glory, and the cycle of abuse continues.

It's sick, really, and while I go through the motions, I'm not as convincing as my brother. It's not long before interested parties move on to asking questions of Coach Marks. Danny still occupies a place in their minds—all they want to know is how I match up against my brother. Which of us is the best.

Clearly uncomfortable, Coach Marks squirms and shifts his weight around before finally demurring: "Danny Bennett was a once-in-a-lifetime athlete and I count myself lucky to have had a chance to work with him. But Gus here is his own swimmer and that means he brings his own unique mind-set and talent to the pool. Don't look to his brother to see what he's capable of. Watch him. And only him."

57.

Watch me.

This is the mind-set I bring back with me to California. Back to everything. I even write it on a piece of paper and tape it to the foot of my bed so it's the first thing I see when I wake up in the middle of the night, and I ride this high straight through the month. The national rankings come out and it's confirmed; I've qualified for Vancouver, meaning I've earned a real shot at qualifying for the Olympic Trials next June.

Well, it would be an understatement to say this steps up the intensity of my training. The intensity of my focus. But this isn't a bad thing. The mounting pressure, the need to perform, it all feels *right*. It all feels like fate of my own making.

My mother is properly awed by my accomplishments and even offers to let me leave school for an online program, which is an opportunity I jump at. She knows what it takes to compete at the level I'm aiming for, and the weak part of me longs to ask if she regrets not letting me swim when I was younger, not letting me chase what Danny wanted. Maybe it would've made us both stronger in the process. To know that she could love us equally despite his talent and in spite of mine. The problem, of course, is that she doesn't.

So I don't say anything.

58.

A few weeks later, I'm busy adjusting my fins in the shallow end before practice one evening, when Raheem and Caleb get into a screaming match over by the outdoor shower. I don't know what sparks it, but I can't say I'm surprised. Something's been brewing between them lately.

Or maybe it's something else, like the fact that this whole process has begun to feel needlessly cruel to my teammates. Now that we are deep into autumn, every practice is cold and dark. In fact, we'll be back here and in the pool before the sun comes up tomorrow morning. Either way, the fight descends into a total shitshow. I look up right as Fitz steps between them, trying to hold them apart. A lost cause, if I've ever seen one; Raheem and Caleb are like pit bulls. More bite than bark and as game as they come. Vince bolts toward the fray but I savor this shit. Half dragging myself from the water, I lie belly down on the pool deck to watch all hell break loose.

"Motherfucker!" Raheem gets a couple swings in, but Caleb laughs and taunts him until Fitz shoves him to the ground. Vince is in the mix by this point, restraining Raheem from kicking Caleb in the goddamn head, and this is when Coach Marks shows up, lumbering in out of nowhere, waving his arms and hollering for everyone to calm the fuck down.

"Are you *kidding* me?" he bellows. "What the *hell* is going on?"

Blood stains the tiles from where Caleb's skinned knees opened up, and Coach M promptly kicks him and Raheem out. I figure the odds are good they'll kill each other in the parking lot. Then Fitz has to get the bleach to clean up the blood, which is a biohazard; I can tell he's pissed about it all and I don't blame him. But I also can't keep the grin off my face.

"Seriously, Bennett?" Coach Marks snaps. "This is funny to you?"

I bite my lip. "Kind of."

"Get in the goddamn water and start warming up."

I do, and it's one of my best workouts ever. I'm electric—this is my proof. I'm not like the other guys, who crumble under pressure. Danny crumbled in spectacular fashion, but for most, failure comes in the form of mediocrity. It's ordinary, which is what I hate about it. Along with all the rationalization about why it's best not to try.

I mean, look, you can tell yourself that taking a day off is self-care or self-compassion or whatever you want in order to justify staying in the same lousy place where you already are. Either way, failure's failure and letting yourself get distracted by girlfriends or egos or shit that's happening online, all it does is take you out of the game and give someone like me an opening.

And it's one I'll take.

Every goddamn time.

59.

Something's not right. I wake up a few days later to find my mother in the kitchen cooking breakfast. It's still dark out—barely five a.m.—but already she's got coffee brewing, a small pitcher of cream out. And she's pulling food from the fridge—eggs, bacon, OJ, the works.

"Hey," I say warily, because this is not a sight I'm used to.

"You want something to eat?" she asks.

"Sure. What's going on here?"

"What does it look like?"

"I have no idea," I say, and it dawns on me why this feels so surreal. Getting up early and making breakfast is something she used to do for *Danny*. Not all the time, but she did it when he was training for something big. Danny loved it, obviously. He loved it anytime he was fawned over and reminded how special he was. My mother played this role for him perfectly. Well, she's probably the one who created his need for adoration in the first place, just so she could fill it. But I have vivid memories of the way she'd grip her mug of coffee, steam spiraling out of it, and watch Danny eat while she hung on every word he said about how much better he was than everyone else.

I get dizzy, thinking about this. There's nothing good in using other people to get what you want, and there's nothing good about being used. But what about people who like being used?

What then?

"I just thought it'd be nice to make you something," my mother tells me. "We haven't spoken in a while. Other than swimming, I don't know what you're up to these days."

I take a seat at the counter. "Where's Winter?"

"Still sleeping."

I nod and watch silently as my mother cracks eggs, slips a pat of sizzling butter into a cast-iron pan. There's an energy to her actions that unsettles me. It's at odds with how *bad* she looks. Her eyes are red and puffy, and her face has aged in some way I can't pinpoint. It's the quality of her skin that's deteriorated—not the color or anything, but the actual texture.

"How's work?" I ask.

She shrugs. Coughs into her elbow. Keeps cooking.

"What does that mean?"

"It means I don't want to talk about it."

"You don't want to talk about work?"

"I need a break from all that, Gus. I'm serious. Too many bitchy brides and mothers-to-be. It's draining my soul."

"But it's your *job*."

"That doesn't mean I have to like it."

"It means you have to do it."

My mother glares at me, all previous cheer gone. "Oh, so you're an expert on life now? Thanks a lot."

"It's common sense!"

"Don't yell at me."

"I'm not *yelling*."

She drops her spatula with a clatter. Gestures at the eggs. "Your breakfast is ready, kid. Don't bother thanking me. I'm going to go lie down."

"Why?"

"Because I can't talk to you right now. I'm too tired for this." She wanders out and while she does indeed look tired, this is her way of ending a conversation she's not interested in having.

I glance at the clock. Five minutes before I have to leave. I wolf down the eggs she's made and a glass of juice with fish oil added to it because I need the fat. Oh, and for all the drama of her exit, my mother doesn't go far. I can hear her coughing in the living room, and I should probably clean up and wash the dishes, since she did cook breakfast for me. That would be an appreciative thing to do, but seeing as she told me not to bother, I don't. I leave everything in the sink for her to find.

60.

Caleb's not on the team anymore. Coach Marks makes this announcement during evening practice, even though it's been like a week since the fight. Raheem's returned with his tail between his legs, so the facts must be on his side. Or maybe Caleb's the one who called it quits on his own. I really don't know and it's not like I have enough goodwill with any of my teammates to just go up and ask.

Either way, his return feels like a bad omen. Not to mention, the workout sucks. Rain starts falling before we get in the water, and in addition to the announcement about Caleb, Coach Marks tells us that the team'll be on hiatus for the next four days due to some family obligation that he has. It sounds like bullshit to me, but everyone else acts like it's some kind of treat to get to sit around on their ass. Well, I vow to make my way out to the Clayton Valley pool every night and every day so that I can train on my own. I've got a schedule to stick to and I'm not letting any obligation get in my way.

Not now.

Not ever.

~~~~~~~~~~

"That was a shitty practice," I grumble to Coach M when we're done. It was worse than shitty, actually. The rain's driving hard, and none of my splits are where they need to be.

"Maybe you need to do less to do more," he offers.

"I don't think it works like that."

He shrugs. "Well, okay, then. I'll see you next week."

Fucking hell. Why does nobody *care*? It's as if I'm all alone in having standards. In wanting to be something more. I march into the changing room and make a beeline for the empty showers because I'm freezing. The hot water is a luxury that turns to torture the instant I step out of it. With a shiver, I bolt for my locker and I'm surprised to see Vince and Raheem and Fitz still hanging out. They're avoiding the rain, I guess, and I don't want to talk to them, but it's hard not to eavesdrop on their conversation when they're standing right next to me.

"Did you see this?" Vince hands his phone to the other two and God knows what they're looking at, but it makes them smile.

"What time should we get there?" Raheem asks.

"Johnny's telling people to come by after eight."

"Can I bring someone?"

"Who?"

"Don't know yet."

"Yeah sure. I mean, I don't care. It'll be packed. Everyone's home for break."

"What break?" I ask without even meaning to. I really don't know what they're talking about.

Fitz turns and gives me a funny look.

"Thanksgiving," Raheem says. "It's Thanksgiving break. You know, for people who actually have to go to school."

"Oh," I say.

"Hey, you should come tonight," Vince says to me. Fitz clears his throat and Raheem looks away, but Vince is undeterred. "I mean it. You should hang with us outside of this pressure shit. It'll relax you a little. You're too tense all the fucking time. It's not healthy."

"Come where?" I ask.

"My brother's throwing a party. He's home from USC and our folks are out of town. Shit'll be crazy. He's kind of a douche but he knows everyone."

"Tonight?"

"We're the last house on Blue Canyon. You know where that is?"

"Yeah."

Vince grins. "So what do you say?"

"I don't know."

"Come on. We don't have practice until Monday. Nothing wrong with having some fun."

"I can't," I say.

"Why not?"

I squirm a little. "Actually, I can. It's just . . . I don't want to."

"Jesus," says Raheem. "Come on, man. That's just rude."

Fitz snorts. "Thanks for the honesty, Bennett."

"What am I supposed to say? I don't like parties."

"It's fine." Vince slips his phone into his pocket and gives me a half smile. "Maybe they don't like you, either. We better get out of here. And, Gus?"

"What?"

"You're not going to tell anyone, right?"

"Like who?"

"Like Coach M."

I shake my head. "About your brother's party? I don't care about that. I just don't want to go."

He sighs. "You already said that."

"I know."

"So we're cool?"

"Yeah," I tell him. "We're cool."

61

My mother's passive-aggressive nature is still going strong by the time I get home. This manifests in her refusing to get off the couch, where she's hunkered down in a pile of blankets, claiming she's sick. Well, her forehead is burning, so it's not total manipulation, but it's sort of the last straw when I end up having to go out again to pick up Winter from her extended-hours day care because they call and ask what the hell is going on.

I consider leaving her there because what's the worst that could happen? CFS takes her and gives her to people who might actually take care of her? But I know I'd never hear the end of it and besides, I don't want to get charged with child abandonment or anything, since I told the person who called that I'd come. My mother's sleeping at this point, with her breath all wheezy and painful sounding.

So I go.

Rain continues to fall as darkness does, too, but fog is the real hazard—reducing visibility to a mere few feet in front of the Mink's headlights. Traffic's cruel this time of night and the two-mile drive to the preschool campus, which is located in the basement of a Presbyterian church out by the wooded Iron Horse Trail, is an exercise in impatience. Cars are sliding every which way or else creeping along like slugs, and I'm nearly rear-ended twice. The second time, it's a truck that almost hits me. It stops so close my throat clenches up, making it hard for me to breathe.

I reach the preschool. Gasping, shaking, I run through the rain into the warm building only to get yelled at and lectured about late fees, even with the extra hours I know my mom pays for. It's nearly seven thirty, and I realize the teachers want to go home but that's no reason to bitch me out. I'm doing them a favor by showing up in the first place.

"The overtime will be on the next bill," one of them says.

"Yeah, I don't deal with that shit," I tell her.

"Yeah, well, that shit is my job," she snaps.

I bite my tongue and grab my niece and shove her into her car seat and get her buckled. She starts crying and her nose is running and she's got a dry cough, so she's probably sick, too, and this day is getting worse by the minute.

Back in the driver's seat. The fog's grown denser and the traffic thicker. I turn music on for Winter, loudly, in part to entertain her and in part to drown out her wailing. A headache hammers behind my skull and a dark sense of doom thrums its way through my nervous system. It sends grim thoughts pinwheeling through my mind:

I want to die.

I hate my fucking life.

Night torments me on the drive back—a thick, snaking darkness that even the fog can't hide. It wants me, I think, and I refuse to turn my head, to look at anything other than taillights in front of me, illuminating wet streaks of red-gold danger. My hands are shaking, but I hold myself together and get us home at last.

I grab Winter, shield her from the rain. I just want to get inside and lock myself away. There's no practice in the morning—I can sleep until three. I can sleep and not wake up again, my traitor brain whispers. With a gasp, I race up the stairs, water dripping into my eyes, before bursting through the front door. Panic nips my heels but I make it. Slam the door behind me.

My mother hasn't moved from the couch and, if anything, looks worse than when I left her. Bad enough to set off alarm bells in my head. Her wheezing's intensified and she can't stop shivering. I clutch Winter to me and feel utterly helpless.

"It's the flu," she croaks. "I need you to get a prescription filled for me. The doctor's called it in."

"What? When?"

"Now. It'll be at the Walgreens on North Main. But you'll have to put Winter to bed first. I can't do it on my own."

62.

I shiver and nod. In her feverish state, I don't think my mom knows what she's asking of me. Putting Winter to bed should be easy. It would be if it didn't involve going upstairs.

For a moment I hesitate, briefly considering allowing my niece to sleep in my bed and my taking the floor. But I'm better than that, I tell myself. At least, I want to be. I turn and walk toward the staircase in the front hallway. In doing so, I adjust Winter's body in my arms, hiking her closer toward my shoulders. She's heavier than I remember, her sleeping head tucked against my chest, and all my dry-land training and conditioning doesn't seem to matter now. The weight pressing down on me is nearly unbearable as I approach the stairs and take the first step. Then the next.

This is how I get there. One labored, miserable step at a time. For all the months I've avoided this journey, I haven't forgotten an inch of it. I haven't been able to. There's the view through the railing. The shadows on the wall. When the second-to-last stair squeaks beneath my feet, I lose it. Sweat starts pouring down my face, and with a gasp I rush forward as best I can, hurrying toward Winter's bedroom in a desperate attempt to outrun the memory of what happened here and what I saw.

My efforts are in vain. The upstairs hallway looms and spins, as distorted as a fun house. As familiar as the truth. I pass what was my bedroom, a small dormered space that once separated me from the rest of my family.

My neck stiffens. Three other bedrooms lie ahead, but I look at nothing but the door to Darien's—now Winter's—as I push my way in. Piles of clothes are heaped on the floor, but I'm confused. Something's different in here. It's the bed, I realize. It's been pulled away from the wall and the window, which isn't how I remember things, but I guess it's safer for Winter this way. She was still in a crib last time I came up here. I walk to the bed, where I lay her down gently, pull her shoes off, and toss a blanket over her. She squirms once, but I stroke her hair, whisper good night.

She settles and I back the hell out of there, pulling the door shut behind me. But it's too late. My mind's caught up with my body, and all my memories come crashing down, threatening to overwhelm me, to keep me locked in timeless despair. I'll always be six and forgotten. I'll always be sixteen and I'll never forget. I slip and catch a glimpse of Danny's room from the corner of my eye. The door's not open and I try and remember whether it was open on that day. The day—

I don't know how it happens, but the next thing I know I'm sitting halfway down the stairs with my head between my knees. *This is bad*, I think. Also: *I can't do this anymore.* But I grip the railing above me and try focusing on the sensation. Wood on skin. The muscles in my arm. Anya from therapy group once mentioned that this was her way of dealing with panic attacks. "Find something in the present and hold on to it," she said. "That's it. That's your anchor. That's all you need to do."

In water, anchors sink, but there are worse things in life, so I follow her advice. I hold the railing and I keep holding it. I keep focusing on where I am and how it feels to exist. The cramping in my knees. The sound of blood rushing to my head. Outside, a gust of wind rattles the house, throws rain against the windowpanes.

"Gus!" my mother calls to me. "What's going on? I need you."

"I'm coming," I mumble. "I'm almost there."

63.

Back in the car. Back in the rain. *She needs me* mixes uneasily with *I hate myself.* But this is who I am. The dutiful son who burns bright with resentment. Although it's possible I've had it backward all this time. Maybe I don't resent all she asks of me while giving me nothing. Maybe I don't let her give me anything, just so I can *be* resentful.

It's what keeps me going, after all.

It's what feeds me.

My brain's addled. Sick. Stuck on an all-too-vivid cycle of what happened in Danny's room the last time I went in there. I hate him for what he did, and I hate myself even more for caring. Control isn't everything in life, but it absolutely should be.

The pharmacy is on the other side of town, and while the traffic's thinned, the rain's grown heavier, slicker. It's a slow ride, sloshing through standing water and battling with the defroster, but I use the time to try to clear my head. I focus on swimming and the fact that I'm less than a month out from Vancouver. It sucks that we're taking a break because Coach Marks has family stuff going on, but there's still a lot I can do on my own. At the moment, I'm less worried about my speed and power than I am about my technique. Something's off about my turns that I can't articulate but need to fix. It's the transitions that make a champion. It's the perfection.

I pull into the Walgreens lot. My head's still prickly, my stomach taut, but I'm damn glad to be here and not on the second floor of our house. Pulling the hood of my sweatshirt up, I exit the car and walk quickly toward the store entrance. Once I'm inside, the sliding doors shut behind me with a hiss, as if I've been consumed. Fluorescent brightness taunts my aching head, but I navigate the aisles of junk food and makeup and diet pills and Squatty Potties and find my way to the pharmacy window. There's a line, a listless staggering that's punctuated by constant coughing. I stand and wait because I have to, and my gaze flits to nearby shelves where I spy everything from allergy medications to enemas to a kit claiming to be both a paternity and ancestry test. That last item feels like some heavy shit to be looking for in a Walgreens.

My turn. I use our insurance card to pay for the Tamiflu and some sort of nasal-related medication. The cashier says the pharmacist wants to consult with me on how to use the second one, but there's no way I'm sticking around. I turn to go, and in the next aisle over I notice a young woman cradling a case of beer in her arms. She's wearing a rain-spattered Oregon Ducks jacket and her dark hair falls below her ears and I freeze at the sight of her—an instinctive response. I know who it is, but it's been so long. I don't know what to do so I just stand there, bag of medicine gripped in one hand, as she heads for the register.

Eventually I trail after her, watching as she pays for the beer, dumps it in a cart, and heads outside. I continue to follow, which feels creepy, but I also can't help myself. In the parking lot she skirts around puddles and walks toward a familiar late-model Ford Explorer packed with other people her age. I can hear them. They're loud, laughing while she loads the beer in the trunk, and she laughs back. Then she gets into the driver's seat. Turns on the ignition.

By this point, I'm on autopilot. I keep my hood pulled tight and sprint across the rain-soaked lot to the Subaru. I'm pretty sure I know where the Explorer's going, and while I didn't want to be there before, suddenly, there's nowhere else I'd rather be.

64.

I hang back so as not to be noticed, and when it's clear where we're going, I hang back even more. The road we're traveling on is twisty, winding high into the hills. I know the way and I know the road, but the swirling ground fog renders the journey near impossible. Visibility is minimal and there are no streetlights up here. I slow the Mink to a crawl, straining to keep track of the guardrail that hovers between me and tragedy.

The road continues to climb as I reach Blue Canyon and cut a left. Trees reach over the road, their shadows dancing dark and long. Coyotes, mountain lions, turkeys live up here. Smaller animals, too, which you can tell in the daylight by the number of crushed bodies strewn across the asphalt.

Soon Blue Canyon splits and the guardrail vanishes, and the road grows narrower, reduced to a single lane. Cars are parked on the left side of the street only, but even those have been maneuvered half onto the sidewalk to keep from being sideswiped. I'm afraid of both hitting vehicles and plummeting over the edge. The fog blows down from the north, gusting against the windshield and swirling over my lights. I don't know which way is up or down. Front or back.

I inch forward because not moving feels more dangerous. More than once, I consider turning around and forgetting this whole thing, but I can't even figure out how to do that, so there's really no choice.

Then finally: lights. Plus dozens of cars, trucks, and SUVs that are jammed along the crumbling cul-de-sac and parked every which way. The house itself is worthy of note—four stories of glass and natural wood that overlook the valley below and the mountains beyond, and I'm kind of stunned to realize I know nothing about Vince or his family or how they came to own a place like this. It has to be worth millions.

Spotting the parked Explorer wedged tight in a space that'll be hell to back out of, I'm gripped with newfound determination. This journey has to mean something. It has to be worth the struggle. So I park against a red curb, not far from a fire hydrant, and step out of the car. Parties have never been my thing—it was true, what I told the guys—although I tagged along with Danny to a few when I was a freshman for the same reason I'm doing it now.

Because I'm weak.

And lonely.

Those parties were always the same. Me forcing down warm beer on an empty stomach and hoping nobody talked to me while Danny played the golden boy—laughing and fist-bumping with everyone he saw. He rarely drank but rarely needed to. There was no social lubrication he didn't already possess, and with his gorgeous girlfriend on his arm, he represented perfection. He had what everyone wanted.

He had what *I* wanted.

All of it.

I head up the drive, long strides, hands in pockets. Light rain spatters my face, my hair, and music streams from the house. The people who are standing outside drinking and smoking seem pretty mellow, although most of them are older than I am. This isn't a typical high school scene, that's for sure.

Once inside I quickly lose my nerve or whatever it is that's brought me here, doggedly chasing down a ghost in a Ford Explorer. *Her*, I don't see. Not anywhere, but it's dark and noisy and bodies are packed tight into every corner.

Sucked through lanes of human traffic, I'm shuttled toward a large room with a vaulted ceiling and a whole wall of windows. It's hard to see where the rest of the house goes. This place is too big. Every angle, every doorway is shrouded with mystery, and every part of me is on edge. But there's nothing to be gained by cutting my losses and I make my way through the crowd.

I push forward as best I can.

65

Moving deeper into the house, I take in all the activity around me: the groups of girls taking photos, the guys playing drinking games. And there's even a couple making out on a white leather couch. The couple intrigues me most, partly because of why I'm here and partly because I've never done any making out of my own. Not for lack of wanting, I guess, but making out with a girl isn't one of those things you get to do just because of wanting.

The guy on the couch gets to do it, though. More than that, even; I watch as he slides his hand inside the girl's shirt, and his hand stays there, just rubbing and touching, making these really small circles on skin I can't see but can intimately imagine. The girl moans a little and I can't help myself; I stop and stare. I stare at them until I get self-conscious about the staring and the fact that people are whispering all around me.

Whispering *about* me.

I walk away, with my eyes glued to the floor and my cheeks on fire and sweat pooling down my back. I stumble into a different room, the kitchen, and the place is wrecked. Food is piled everywhere, and I sidestep what appears to be a spilled bowl of fruit salad. Someone hands me a bottle of Wild Turkey like it's a trophy, only I don't know what I'm supposed to do with it. I don't want to ask, so I pour some into a plastic cup. When the cup's nearly full, I dump in what I can from a bottle of diet cream soda to cover up the taste and the smell and even though I know better, I'm also desperate and I drink the whole thing as fast as possible.

I drink more after that because my heart's pounding and besides, isn't alcohol supposed to get you to relax? That's not a skill set I have or value normally, and the Wild Turkey *does* tame my nerves a hair. The physical stuff, at least, but my mind is unstoppable, churning with an overabundance of data. My goal is to find *her*, but all I can think about is the fact that I was only invited to this party as a way to keep me from snitching. No one wants me here and why would they? I'm in the middle of pouring another drink as more people crash into the kitchen, flooding the room with laughter, and I cringe a little, realizing that they're from Acalanes, my old high school.

"Hey," I say, because it's the polite thing to do. But the newcomers ignore me. They're too focused on getting their own cups, their own drinks. A girl I know from chemistry class—we were partners last year—bumps my elbow at some point, sloshing my drink onto my shirt.

She turns, giggles. "Sorry."

"It's okay," I say, but she's turned away already and there's no flicker of recognition in her eyes.

For a moment I stay where I am, leaning against the center island like it's keeping me from being lost at sea. But the divide in the room is clear. There's them.

And there's me.

Everything starts to spin. I grab my cup and bolt, ricocheting down a hallway I don't recognize in pursuit of fresh air. Apparently this is what being drunk is like, and I don't know where the relaxed and happy idea comes from. That's the opposite of how I feel, but maybe it's *me* that's not working properly, not the booze, so I really shouldn't be pointing any fingers.

There are too many stairs in this house. I go down a floor and find myself in some hot-as-Hades utility room where a bare lightbulb swings from the ceiling and someone's DJ-ing and I think people are getting ready to rap. My instinct is to back out of there quickly, but before I do I catch sight of Raheem and *Caleb* of all people standing in the corner. The two of them glance up together, catch my eye, and I know they see me. Caleb leans in to whisper something in Raheem's ear and they both break out laughing.

Fuck. I march back up the stairs and then go up another flight. I pass a girl crying on the stairs and another girl attempting to console her. I peer at them both, to see if I know them. One of the girls has curly red hair—not the crying one—and she reminds me of Lynette from grief group, the one who let her little brother slip beneath the water in his bath when she ran to get a towel. But it can't be her. She's too young for all this. *Is* it her? The staircase is too dark and it's too hard to make out faces. I creep closer, hoping for a better look, and that's when one of the girls hisses at me, like an actual cat, and I scamper away, stumbling, spilling more of my drink.

Upstairs is worse. It's a wide room with sliding doors that open to a foggy deck adorned with burning candles. Hundreds of them. Everyone turns and looks at me, like maybe this is some sort of VIP area or a place losers like me aren't meant to access. At this point, I'm too freaked to keep running up and down the stairs, so I huddle in the hallway, cup in hand, with my back glued to the wall, and I let the pulsing bass from two floors below vibrate through my body.

Then Vince finds me. I don't know how this happens. One minute I'm alone and the next he's standing in the hallway with me, laughing and pouring something else into my cup.

"Drink!" he says. And I do.

"When the fuck did you get here?" he hollers.

"Not that long ago," I say. "Nice house!"

"Thanks. I thought you weren't interested in coming!"

I shrug.

"You always this shy, Bennett?" Vince shouts.

"I think I'm drunk," I shout back. "It's not shyness."

He shakes his head. "I don't mean now. I mean all the time. The guys are always wondering what's up, you know? Like you never hang with us. We're not cool enough for you or something?"

"That's not it," I say. "I just want to do well in Vancouver. It's important to me. It's everything."

Vince leans his shoulder against the wall. "Doing well is important to me, too. Doesn't mean you can't have friends."

"But we're—we're competitors," I say, surprising myself with my honesty. "How can we be friends?"

"Seriously?"

"Seriously."

A loose smile breaks across Vince's face. "Nah, man. We're teammates. We're a team. We all help each other out. Got it?"

I nod vigorously, but um, no, I don't get it. Vince's words sound stupid, like the kind of shit people *say* but never mean. At the end of the day, only one of us is going to hit that wall first and it might as well be me. It *will* be me. But I know better than to speak my mind right then, because the truth is, I feel a whole lot better standing drunk in the hallway with Vince than I did when I'd been standing here alone. So maybe being close to people isn't such an awful thing.

Or is that just mediocrity talking?

I rub my chest. God. Life isn't *supposed* to be this hard. Parties are supposed to be fun. Everyone always acts like they're the best thing ever. Like they're just what you *do* when obligations like school and studying and practice don't get in the way, because why the hell would you be doing anything else? But I don't know. To me, *this* is work. Swimming's easy compared to *this*. Winning's easy, too.

Vince takes a long swallow from his cup. Smacks his lips loudly.

"So what're you drinking?" I ask, because I need grounding, an anchor. The floor beneath me feels like it's sliding away.

"Screwdriver," Vince says. "That's—"

"Vodka and orange juice," I finish. "My mom drinks those."

"Yeah? What's she like?"

"A total bitch."

Vince laughs and tips his cup at me.

I take this as an invitation to keep talking. "She hates me, you know. She used to tell me that when I was a kid."

"That's messed up."

"She only ever loved Danny and my sister sort of, but she treats me like shit. Always has. My whole fucking life."

"Why?"

"Because I killed my father."

Vince nods and laughs again. He's not looking at me, I realize. No, a pretty girl walking back from the bathroom is coming right toward him. She stops, leans against the wall. The girl has swaying hair, swaying hips, and a crop top that shows off her belly and stretches across her chest in a heartbreaking way.

She says something to Vince and he says something back. Soon he's touching her, and I watch, baffled, as he sets his hand on her wrist and strokes her skin like it's nothing. Soft skin, it looks so soft. I don't get how Vince has the nerve to do it, but in response, the girl tosses her hair and smiles. I stare at both of them, but I also don't want to stare. I haven't forgotten what happened earlier when I saw that couple making out on the couch and the way it made me feel.

The way people had started to *whisper*.

My head's spinning again, and soon there are two Vinces, then four, then six. Overhead a light flickers, and Vince and the pretty girl keep spinning and spinning and spinning. Then it must be the Wild Turkey doing stuff to me because I physically can't keep from speaking my mind.

"I'm haunted," I say out loud.

"What was that, Bennett?" Vince asks.

"I think I'm being haunted."

66.

Someone is after me.

Or something.

I steal a glance over my shoulder, into the cold night. My breath comes in short bursts, tight puffs of white air. I see nothing behind me except shadows, but I heard the footsteps. I know this. Or maybe not *footsteps*, exactly, but . . . almost. I turn back around and walk faster. I've made it down the drive and into the street, and my car can't be far. I have to be getting close, although it's hard to tell in all the soupy haze. It feels as if I've been walking in this frigid air forever. Initially leaving the party had felt good, like freedom, like I could breathe again, even though my legs are wobbly and my stomach kind of hurts. I didn't tell Vince I was leaving, but he wouldn't care. Why would he? He was still with that girl, pressed up against the wall, screwdriver gripped tightly in one hand, and the rest of my teammates, well, I have no clue where they might be. And I really don't care.

God, why did I say that about being haunted?

A little voice inside my head answers.

(because it's true.)

I keep moving, but my stomach starts to hurt more, like a sharp pain.

Don't get sick, I tell myself. *Please. Just keep walking, keep walking.*

I look over my shoulder again.

Still nothing. Just shadows. Black ones. But as my jittery gaze darts across the foggy asphalt, something *moves*. I gasp. Whatever it is, its movement is almost inky, a shadow coming to life, oozing down the path, heading straight for me.

I turn and bolt. And run right into somebody.

"Gus!" she says brightly. "I found you."

I'm too startled to speak but I know who it is and I don't know how she found me or even why she might have been looking in the first place. She is looking for me, right? That's what it means to want to find someone, although it also means I've been lost.

I think I'm still lost.

"Lainey," I manage. And there's so much more I need to say, so much inside me that's been stuck for so long, waiting for this moment I never believed would come. The words don't come, though, and I just stare at her, frozen.

"What's wrong?" she asks. "You look weird."

"S-someone was chasing me."

"Someone?"

"Something?"

She peers behind me. "I don't see anything."

"I guess it's gone now," I say, but I start to shiver. From the cold. From fear. But Lainey's bolder than I am. She takes me in her arms and murmurs how damn happy she is to see me.

"I saw you in the kitchen earlier," she whispers. "But then you ran out and I couldn't find you again. I was looking everywhere."

"Why?" I croak.

"What do you mean, *why*?"

"Why were you looking for me?"

"I've wanted to talk to you ever since—you know. I'm sorry I couldn't come to the funeral. I wanted to so badly but I couldn't get back in time. Then I thought you'd be at the dedication thing for Danny's scholarship, but . . ." She trails off, her eyes soft, pooling with tears. "How're you doing?"

I shake my head.

"I'm sorry. That's what I wanted to tell you. Not that he's gone, although I'm sorry for that, too. But how it happened. What you had to go through. That wasn't fair."

I shiver more. I can't explain it, but I've waited so long for someone to say what she's saying and to understand how I feel. That's it not just that my brother died. And it's not just that he killed himself.

But *how*.

Lainey's the only person who could really understand, I think. She loved him once and he broke her heart, and even after, she still cared for him as a person and as a friend. That drove me crazy, but she was my friend, too, and I've always loved her. I've never stopped. Not since the moment I met her when Danny brought her home after practice one night. I was thirteen and she was seventeen, and together we sat on the back porch while he showered and changed. That's a night I've never forgotten. Beneath the stars and the moon, we talked for what felt like hours about siblings and loneliness and our shared love of solitude. From then on, Lainey went out of her way to be my friend. Even when Danny told her not to bother because I was sullen and callous and would probably grow up to be a serial killer, and that's if I was lucky. Anyway, I know there's no hope for any romantic connection between us— there never has been—but the longer she hugs me, holds my body to hers, I can't help but want.

"Gus," she whispers again. "Oh, sweet boy. You didn't do anything wrong, okay?"

But I did, I want to tell her.

"You don't deserve this. You don't have to hate yourself."

But I do.

"Do you miss him?" I ask.

"Every day."

"But why? You weren't even together when . . ."

"He should be here. He had his whole life ahead of him."

"He didn't want his life."

"He was sick. Very, very sick. You know that as well as I do."

I grit my teeth. Close my eyes. And it's the strangest thing. I can hear the footsteps again. The ones following me earlier. I hear them. Growing louder. Getting closer. Only I'm fairly certain that if I were to turn around, there would be nothing there. That the footsteps are coming from inside *me*.

I shudder. Back away.

"Shhh," Lainey says. "Gus. It's okay. Stay with me. You're doing fine. You're fine. However you feel, it's okay."

But I can't stay. That's the thing. That's what wrong. What's always been wrong.

"I'm sorry," I tell her, and I am. What's wrong. I really, really am. *Sorry.*

67.

I'm driving again, which is beyond stupid and I *know* that, but I have to get out of here. I shouldn't have come in the first place. I shouldn't have let my guard down and invited weakness into my life. This is what temptation gets you. Wanting to touch some goddamn flame whose heat was never mine to begin with.

Fuck.

Forgive me, Lainey.

Please forgive me.

The fog's cleared enough that the road is visible, and I throw on my high beams as I make my way back down into the canyon below. My stomach's knotting and my hands are sweating and this, this is what I get for taking my eyes off the prize, for not keeping swimming a hundred percent in my focus. That voice is in my head again, the one I heard earlier, and it's whispering other, worse things now:

Jerk the wheel.

And

You're worthless.

And

Go ahead and do it, you pussy. Follow in Danny's fucking footsteps already.

And finally

Isn't that what you want?

Isn't that what you've been doing?

"No," I snarl, and maybe it's crazy but I'm already past the point of no return, and I know what it is that I need to do. I know what will get these fucking voices out of my head once and for all and keep me where I need to be.

Upon reaching the bottom of the canyon, I pull over and leave the engine idling. It's easy enough to lean across to the passenger side, although the damn car slides forward and I panic, flailing for the brake.

Heart pounding, I put the damn thing in park, reach for the glove compartment, and grab what I'm looking for: the envelope Danny left behind. I plug the address into my phone's GPS—ignoring the fact that my mom's called like eight times in the past couple hours—and then I'm heading for the highway and I don't look back. That's how eager I am to leave that bullshit party far, far behind me.

68.

Alamo. I'm heading to Alamo.

This is the reverse trip my father made on the day he died, and it's the one I'm making now in order to stay alive. Okay, that's dramatic, but it's also how I feel and even though I'm not one to put much stock in shit like signs or coincidences, this has all the makings of destiny.

How could it not?

Unlike that long-ago day when I put my mother in the hospital before I was even born, there's no traffic this time of night. Nothing to slow me down or keep me from my fate. The foothills are on my right, hulking shadows against the gloomy sky. There's no moon. No nothing but the dim lights of the cars in front of me and the occasional fluorescent strip-mall glow. I ride the fast lane out through Walnut Creek, Danville, and finally into Alamo, a suburb known for its ostentatious wealth and giant homes, and no, I don't worry about getting pulled over, getting busted, losing fucking everything I ever thought I had. I'm invisible tonight.

I know this.

I know this to be true.

It's exactly what's brought me here.

69

The navigation system tells me what exit to get off at and where to go. The streets in Alamo are different than Lafayette's crooked and abstract tree-lined ones. Here the boulevards are wide, well-lit, clean, and predictable. Trees are planted in measured increments and rather than just street names at every corner, each neighborhood has its name written on a plaque with curly letters. Windemere. Stone Valley. West Gate. Alamo Meadows.

I'm instructed to turn right into Crosswind Farms, which has neither wind nor farms from what I can tell. The houses here are massive, all built with a Spanish Colonial flair—cream stucco and red tile roofs with lush green lawns that don't give the impression that any drought rationing has been happening in this zip code. I mean, it hasn't. That's obvious. Just down the road from here is the infamous Blackhawk neighborhood—once home to John Madden and that guy from Mötley Crüe—which is not only gated but used to have its own grocery store featuring a man in tux and tails playing a grand piano. People like that don't ration.

The house I'm looking for is indistinguishable from the ones around it, but the architecture, the landscape, the lighting, everything there is crafted to be inviting. I find it finally and pull to the curb and sit in the idling car, which is a surefire way to get the cops called on me, or worse. But it's hard for me to get out. To do what I came here to do.

Another call from my mom comes through and I don't answer, because why the fuck does she get to need me when it suits her?

Everything's always about her. It always has been. She calls again and I do it. What I've dreamt of doing for as long as I can remember. I pull up her number and hit block.

My mouth fills with spit and I push the door open just in time to puke all over the street. Also the side of the car, which is fucking great. At least I have the motivation to finally move my ass or else I really will end up in jail. I wipe my mouth, step carefully out of the car, and approach the house, with its wide cobblestone walkway and neat path of perfect copper lighting. I kick at one of the lights, then kick it again, just to watch it flicker out.

A dog barks from inside, a low throaty sort of utterance. I try bounding up the steps only to trip and bang my shin hard. It's a chore getting up again, but then I'm knocking on the door. Pounding because it's hard to imagine anyone inside can hear me. Then I spy one of those fancy brass knockers that's in the shape of a mermaid, which gets me to roll my eyes, but I switch to that, banging even harder with the added weight.

No answer.

"Fuck me," I mumble, and I take a step back and look up at the house. Three whole stories spin wildly, and I straighten up before I fall over. It strikes me as a good idea, however, to throw something at one of the upper windows, which must be the bedrooms. That'll be more productive than banging on a first-floor door that doesn't even have a fucking bell.

I bend over and inspect the stone porch for anything I can use. There's nothing, so I back down the stairs and fumble around in the flower beds. They're immaculate, of course, lush with neat rows of blooms, even in November. But my fingers grasp a good-sized river rock and I heft it once in my palm, making sure it's of adequate weight, which it is. Then I set my jaw, lift my arm, pull back, and that's when I hear it. A voice. It says:

"You better think real hard about if you want to do that, son."

70

I falter, confused. Is this voice inside my head or out? But then the porch light comes on and I spot a silhouette of a man walking straight toward me.

I breathe a sigh of relief. "Coach Marks!"

"*Gus?*"

"Yeah."

"What're you doing here?"

"I need to talk to you."

"Talk about what?" Coach Marks approaches and we're both standing there on his lawn and he's wearing a robe and glasses and he doesn't really look like how I remember him even though I only saw him this evening. Well, technically yesterday evening, now, but that sounds weird seeing as I haven't slept or anything since. Plus, I'm panting, I realize with a strange wave of awareness.

"Training," I say. "For Vancouver."

"*That's* what you want to talk to me about? Now?"

"Well, we're only three weeks out and I feel like I'm ready. I got this. I fucking know I do."

"You all right, Gus?"

"Yeah, I'm good. But see, it doesn't make sense that we're not practicing again until Monday. Now's when we need to push— look, maybe I haven't told you that before, but it's what I need. To be pushed. Hard. I know I can be . . . difficult, but I can do anything you tell me to. I can do more, even. I can be epic. But you just need to get me there. Okay?"

He doesn't move. I stand there, gasping for breath, and hear the *whip whip whip* of sprinklers from somewhere down the block.

"Why don't you come inside?" he offers gently. "It's late."

"I don't want to come inside!" I shout. "I need *answers*! You're my coach. You told Danny how to do it. Now tell me!"

"Okay," he says, walking toward me. "I'll tell you. I'll give you answers. Right now you need rest. I think you might need more than that, but taking some time off from swimming will be a good start."

"Fuck that," I say. "That's the last thing I need."

He takes another step. "You think I don't know about all the extra training you do on your own at the pool in the valley? You think it's going to help if you get yourself injured before Vancouver? Or to overtrain? Your splits aren't getting any better and you know it. That means you need to back off before you move forward. But because you won't listen to me when I tell you what's best for you, scheduling days off might be the only way I have to save you from yourself. Although I doubt it."

"So you *lied* to me?"

"No, I didn't lie. The truth is that I'd rather spend time with my family for the holiday. Maybe you should do the same."

"Is that what you told Danny? That he should take time off when he felt like it?"

"I should have."

"You don't mean that."

His eyes blaze. "You think I don't *mean* that? You think I don't wish that I'd done things differently with him? That I know I shouldn't have pushed him like I did?"

"He wanted you to push him. It's all he wanted."

"That doesn't make it right."

My lip curls. "Well, then I hope he suffered. I hope he felt what he made me feel that day. The way he still makes me feel. I hope it hurt like hell, what he did to himself. He deserved it."

"Jesus," he breathes. "Don't say that, Gus. I know you're hurting, but don't ever, ever say that."

"Fuck you! Stop caring about him more than you care about me!" And with that, I rear back and hurl the river rock as hard as I can at one of those wide leaded windowpanes on the second floor. The sound of shattering glass is deafening.

I whirl to face his rage. It's lit by the motion-activated flood-light and scored by the now-shrieking alarm system. There's no kindness left. No concern.

"Get out!" he bellows. "Get the hell out of my sight!"

71.

He realizes his mistake an instant later and lunges after me, apologizing, begging me to come inside. Not to leave, for God's sake, or get behind the wheel. He's fast. But I'm faster. I jump in my car, hit the gas, and leave.

Well, shit. That episode kind of cleared my head and made me see what was true all along. I can't trust anyone with my future. No one's really on my side but me, and so I'll do it all myself if no one's willing to coach me. If no one's willing to push me where I need to be and let me be better than the one force on this earth who worked the hardest to keep me down. I drive even faster on my way back to Lafayette and I roll the window down to keep myself awake.

To keep myself afire.

I make it to the LCC. Both the places I have memberships to are closed, but this is the one with the standard-sized pool and that's what I need. Time for some breaking and entering again. It's barely one a.m., and I don't have my suit or a towel or goggles or anything. But this doesn't stop me. At this point, nothing will. Scaling the fence is a trickier proposition now that I'm drunk and my shin's bleeding from when I fell earlier, but I make it over somehow, although I slip the last bit and slam onto the dirt below. I land on my side with a *whoof*, which knocks the wind out of me but I don't waste time looking up at the sky or lamenting my pain. No, I'm up again in an instant, heading for the aquatic center, stripping off my clothes and bounding for the water's edge.

I dive deep. There's solace in the cold, the discomfort, in having to force myself to keep moving so that I don't sink slowly to the bottom. It's the only way to stay alive, isn't it? When I was a kid our school took a trip to the aquarium in Monterey, where they were trying to keep a great white shark in captivity but the damn thing wouldn't swim. They stuck a diver in there with it to push the shark forward, to keep the air flowing through its gills, and endlessly spiral through the murky tank. It was futile, though. The shark died the next day. I read about it online and couldn't understand why the aquarium had even tried to keep it in the first place. Some people would call that hope, I guess, but it seemed like cruelty to me.

I ease into my warm-up, keeping my strokes crisp and sharp. Alcohol's no excuse for poor form. It's no excuse for anything. And see, Coach Marks was right, in a way. I haven't been lowering my split times. Not to where I need them to be, and it's not for lack of trying. But maybe it's for lack of support. Or guidance. Or a lack of fucking faith. He's always loved Danny more and, whether consciously or not, he can't stand the fact that I'm better than my brother. Just like he can't stand the fact that my brother left him.

Sufficiently warm, I crawl from the water, teeth chattering, bones shaking, and my wet feet slap on tile as I dart to the utility shed to retrieve one of the starting blocks. I know where the key's kept, so that's no problem, but once I'm in the shed, the blocks are stacked together and heavy and difficult to maneuver on my own, and pretty soon I thank God for the gusting wind. It masks the noise of me clambering around in there for what I need. Finally, I'm able to grasp the block in my arms. With a grunt and a groan, I drag it back to the deep end and shove it into the mount.

Click.

Up on the block, I shiver harder, but this is it. My time that I've made happen because no one else fucking will and this is my chance to get a sub-1:47 time on my 200 m free. I stare first at the clock on the other side of the pool, that sweeping red second hand, then down into the murky depths.

Time and the elements: both are my mortal enemies. I hold my breath, and at the top of the minute I go, launching myself through the air, determined to destroy both.

On my terms.

01:49.23.

    Fuck.

    I go again.

    01:48.33.

    Again.

    01:48.21.

    Again.

    01:49.24.

    Again.

    01:50.27.

    Again.

    01:49.23.

    Again.

    01:49.34.

    Again.

    Again.

    Again.

    Again.

73.

I don't know what I notice first: the bloodstains—dark streaks of crimson—or the sun peeking over the horizon, a smooth orangey glow. I'm standing on the block, more sweat dripping off me than water, and when I bend down, the blood's everywhere, lit by the sun, and jagged pieces of flesh gape from my heels.

My knees sway at the sight. It's clear what the source is: blisters worn raw and then some. I deserve it, though. The pain. I've been at this all night and have nothing to show for it but failure.

I give it one more go. My feet throb now that I've noticed them, and my dive is determined but off-center. I hit the water wrong, but that doesn't stop me. Every chance is a chance to make it right. A chance for redemption. But my stroke won't come easy. I picture the trail of blood in my wake and the dying shark at my heels. I kick and pull and breathe and kick, but it's no use and this is where hope dies, I guess. Not in my surrender but my ineptitude.

I hit the wall.

Look at the clock.

01:54:12.

Chest heaving, muscles trembling, I make my way toward the diving pool with its twelve-foot drop. With all its pressure. The platform calls to me. Twenty-five feet up. I use all four limbs to climb the ladder, and my bloody footprints offer a rush of contentment. I've left my mark in some way. That has to count for something.

I reach the top. Look around. The sun's breaking through the clouds, lighting up the whole club—the glittering golf course and immaculate grounds. It's whisper quiet, which surprises me. Even without swim practice there are usually people here, hitting balls, jogging, heading to the fitness center. But the place is empty. No cars. Nothing.

The breeze rustles through my hair. The chalky dusk grows brighter and maybe I'm asleep or at the bottom of the pool or the entire world population died while I was swimming and I'm the only survivor. I don't think I'd mind. The quiet. The peace. This is what I relish. What I'm seeking. I walk to the end of the platform. Gingerly step on wounded feet, and I can't help but wince. The pain's broken through by now.

My toes curl around the edges of the rigid platform, and I risk a glance at the depths below. My head sways at the sight and my muscles tense in an effort to hold me back. To keep me from falling.

But it's too late. My strength is gone. Or else gravity is just the better competitor this morning. I don't doubt it.

And at this point, I simply don't care.

75.

Crumpling like I do and hitting the water from that height and that position is akin to crashing through glass. My bones and body smack hard, erupting with pain and brokenness, and then I'm sinking, sinking, submerged.

Sunk.

My eyes sting when I open them. My lungs burn. Every part of me aches inside and out. Every part of me has been hurting for a long time, I realize. And I'm sick of this pain, more than anything, but the longer I stay under, the more my pain's replaced with a rocketing sort of euphoria. Of wild tumbling *need*. It fills me up in a way I haven't been filled in a long time, and there's a passion to dying, I think. To ending one's suffering, and maybe this is what Danny was chasing more than death itself.

Not the end so much, but the *anticipation*.

Is this what he felt with that belt tightening around his neck?

A certain sort of grace?

I'll never know, I guess, because I'm not Danny. My passion's more pragmatic than his. He was fire where I'm all ice. Or else my spite's too strong. My method too weak. So as I hover at the point of no return, that place where my lungs can no longer bear the pressure of this pool, its depths, I turn and kick.

And kick.

And kick.

Daybreak.

I'm driving home because I don't know who or what I am anymore. The sun's rising in the sky, having burned off all the fog, and I'm driving home because even though everything's changed, nothing has, and so I'm driving home because I know I always will.

77.

Winter.

She's the first thing I hear when I drag myself into the house. It's not her normal pissed-off baby screaming to be fed or pick me the fuck up or love me for once, goddammit. No, this is a different sound. A gurgling one. Like she's choking.

I bolt forward. The sound is coming from the kitchen and this is where I find her, stuck in her high chair but struggling to get out. She's managed to slip halfway out of the harness, sliding partway under the tray and catching her neck against the seat while her tiny body dangles a good foot above the floor. She thrashes and cries out more and I grab her, unclip the harness, and pull her to safety.

"You're okay," I say breathlessly. "You're fine, baby." The words provide more reassurance for me than her, but she *is* fine other than her fear. Her anger. My fingers run along the red line where the strap was pressed across her throat. It's not a bad mark. She wasn't in true danger, I don't think, but why was she in any at all? Her wails ease as I rock her and soon she quiets enough to grab my chin, touch my hair.

"Gusssss," she coos, and while she may have recovered, I'm suddenly furious. Adrenaline floods my body and I get that accidents happen, but this is inexcusable. She's a baby. Helpless.

She could've *died*.

Red heat fills me. I march through the sunlit house, shouting for my mother to account for what she's done. You don't take on the care of a child if you aren't going to *care*. Darien knew that.

She knew enough not to pretend and wear a mask of motherhood, because that's even crueler than abandonment. All it does is teach a child they aren't deserving of love.

My mother doesn't answer. This enrages me more, enough that it pushes back my fear and lets me pound right up the stairs to the second floor in search of her. After last night, after all I did, I'm ready to tear shit down. I'm ready to burn.

I don't find her in her room—a quiet space with oak furniture handed down from her parents and walls lined with her photography, images that have always shown me how she sees the world and what in it matters most to her. Almost all are of Danny throughout the years, but I'm startled to find a framed photo of me hanging over her dresser. I can't be older than ten or eleven in the shot and no, I'm not swimming but at least it's of me alone—not me and Danny or even Darien. I'm reading a book and I've tucked myself beneath an antique side table that sits in our living room. There's a vent there, and I used to plant my butt on it in the winter as a means of stealing the heat before anyone else could get it.

Did she put this photo of me up before or after Danny died? I suspect after, and a wave of pride stamps my heart with a fierceness I don't even try to suppress. Because this photo says there's still a way for me to be better than him in her eyes. For me to replace him, bit by bit, memory by memory.

A sick grin crosses my lips only to vanish as my stomach weakens. I know what's going to happen and I let Winter slip from my arms to the bed before lurching to the master bath in search of a place to vomit, which I find. But I also find my mother. She's sprawled flat on the tile floor, her face pale, her eyes rolled back, and blood's pooled around her head.

With a whimper, I go to her, to do what I can, but I don't know how or even what's wrong. Her breathing's labored, raspy, and her skin's hot, and now I remember the flu medicine I never brought back. It's still in the car where I tossed it after deciding to follow Lainey. This is my fault. All my fault. My eyes sting and finally, I fumble for my phone, dial 911, and whimper something tragic until they tell me help is on the way, that they'll be there, that, sir, they need me to calm down.

Then I wait with Winter and I hold her close, as close as I can, because I need that, the closeness. More than she does, even.

78

The sirens wail.

I rush downstairs to greet them. I repeat what I know, which isn't much, and they take it from there. I mostly feel numb because I've done this before and I'll probably have to do it again some other time. We're a family of tragedy. Doomed, you could say. But at least help is here and the first responders who show up are actually doing something. Assisting my mom and talking to her. Not like last time when it was already too late.

"She's dehydrated," one of the EMTs, a woman with dark hair and glasses, comes and tells me after a few minutes of checking vitals and running tests. "Probably passed out and that's how she cut her head. Her lungs sound pretty rheumy, too. Might be pneumonia."

"She's had the flu. She was at the clinic yesterday."

"It's going around. Bad this year."

"Is she going to be okay?"

"She's stable but needs fluids. Stitches. Maybe a breathing treatment and monitoring for any secondary infection. We'll take her in to John Muir, and the doctors there can give you more information once they've had a chance to evaluate her condition."

I feel panicky. "But what am I supposed to do? Don't I need to do something? Do I come with you?"

She glances at Winter. "What's your name?"

"Gus."

"How old are you, Gus?"

"Seventeen."

"Do you have any family you can call?"

"No."

"Neighbors you're close with?"

"Not really."

"And whose baby is this? Is she yours?" She smiles at Winter, who curls her head against my chest and hides her face.

"She's my sister's kid. But she's . . . she's not around."

"What about the father?"

I shake my head.

"Then I'll call Child and Family Services for you, okay? They'll come out. They'll know what to do."

My legs feel weak. "They won't take her, will they? They won't take her away?"

"They'll make sure you're both safe." Her voice is soothing, firm. "You doing okay, hon? You don't look too good."

"No. I don't know."

"What's wrong?"

I shake my head again. The numbness inside me is giving way to something else. "It's my fault. I . . . I was supposed to get her medicine last night and I didn't. I went out and I didn't come home and now this happened!"

The EMT's expression shifts from sad to startled to helpless. All in an instant.

"It's not your fault," she says.

"It is!"

She sighs. "I remember you, you know. From last spring. I was on that call. That was hard, what happened to your brother."

I nod.

"I'm real sorry you had to go through that alone."

My whole body's shaking now. I grip Winter tight like she's the one holding me together. "I deserved it, though, didn't I? Having to find him like that? This kind of proves it."

The woman turns and walks away from me. No doubt she's sick of my shit the way I'm sick of it, too. I watch her talk to her partner and they get my mom loaded into the ambulance and switch the lights on, but not the siren.

Then she comes back to where Winter and I are huddled by the staircase. She stands closer than I'm comfortable with.

"Your mom's going to John Muir now," she says.

"Okay."

"But I'm going to stay with you two until CFS arrives."

"You will?"

"Sure. Do you think that baby will let me hold her?"

"Her name's Winter."

"Pretty name." Winter peeks out at the woman, her smiling face, her open arms. It takes her a moment, but she goes to her. And it's weird how it's a load off my arms but it also makes me feel like crap. Like nobody wants me.

Like nobody ever will.

"Thank you," I say, because no matter how deep my self-pity, this woman's doing me about a million favors. "For everything."

She smiles. "I figure it's the day for that."

"What?"

"It's Thanksgiving," she says. "Today. You know that, right?"

79.

The ambulance leaves, and I watch it go and I feel awful. It's not that I want to be with my mother. I don't, in fact. Not one bit.

But I also don't want her to be alone.

Not now.

Not like this.

Part
Three

Fuck.

81.

You want to know what I really and truly hate about my life?
Everything.

"Sit down," the EMT says when I won't stop pacing the living room, the hallway. I obey by flopping my ass down on the couch beside her and Winter, who's watching something on the Disney Channel. It's obnoxious but I envy her this distraction because my mind won't stop spinning, a sickly turn of memories that wash over me, again and again, ensuring that I remember every mortifying detail of the night before. The party. The girl. The coach.

My mother.

A moan escapes me and with that, I'm up again, wringing my hands, marching back and forth. If being still with myself isn't the answer, something else sure as hell must be. That's what I've always believed; that no matter how close to the bottom you're scraping, there's always hope, if you rely on your own wits. There's always a way out.

Winter laughs at some talking animal on the screen and a clammy sweat breaks out on the back of my neck. What if CFS tries to take her from me? What if I lose her? Maybe I should just take her and go right now. We could get in the car and start driving to Mexico, like in some bad indie movie. We might make it, although hell, the cops would probably be after me in an instant—not just for kidnapping, but when they find out what I did in Alamo last night.

I grab my phone and call the hospital to get an update on my mother. No one at the front desk will tell me anything, and I freely tell them how much I think they fucking suck. It's not until after two p.m. that a doctor *finally* calls back and says my mother's being treated for pneumonia and a mild concussion.

"But she'll be okay?" I ask.

"She's stable at the moment. We should know more tomorrow."

"Will she be there long?"

"At least a few days." She gives me the extension to the room where my mother is staying, although I'm not sure what I'm supposed to do with this information. It's not like I plan on calling her and I'm fairly certain the sentiment goes both ways, although I realize my mother must've authorized the phone call from the doctor. But is this kindness on her part?

Or a power play for my well-owed guilt?

My stomach cramps and as soon as I hang up I have to run to the bathroom to puke *again*. I barely make it but there's nothing left in me. The endless retching just leads to pain and more pain. Soon I'm kneeling on the floor, with sweat running down my face, and my bastard mind starts listing off the lethal options lurking in the medicine cabinet above me. No, this isn't the first time I've had thoughts like these, but I've never acted on them. Well, not really. And it's one of the ways I know I'm a stronger person than Danny.

Then again, maybe I'm not.

The front doorbell rings. I strain to listen as the EMT answers. She murmurs something I can't make out as my stomach heaves again. It could be the cops for all I know, but I'm bent over the toilet and I can't move and for once in my life, I'm resigned to my fate. Someone knocks on the bathroom door and I don't say anything. Whoever it is will break it down, I figure. They'll get to me. Only they knock again and then the door just opens. I turn to look, bracing myself, only it's not the cops or CFS.

It's Coach Marks.

83.

"What're you doing here?" I'm vaguely horrified to see that a woman I recognize as Coach Marks's wife is with him. She looks . . . unnerved.

"What do you think we're doing?" he says gruffly as he kneels beside me, holding me steady. "You're coming to stay with us."

That's not a question and I can't run away from him like I did last night, so I just nod. It takes time, however, before I can stand again without feeling queasy and in the interim, Coach Marks does nice things like bring me water and put a cool washcloth on my forehead. He also tells me about his first hangover and how his father made him get up at six a.m. and mow the lawn as punishment. I wish I could say his kindness made me feel better or cared for, but the opposite is true. When I am able to move around again, I agree to pack clothes for myself but have to confess to being unable to go upstairs and get stuff together for Winter.

Coach M's wife appears startled by this admission but tells me not to worry about it. My eyes water when she says this because she has to know what I did to her house last night. She has to know how awful a person I am.

Coach Marks is in the living room talking with the EMT when I return from packing. The conversation between them looks intense, but I can't make out their words. I mumble that I'm ready to go or whatever. The EMT nods and tells me she's leaving now, and I let her hug me, even though I hate hugs, and

I thank her because I really and truly am grateful for what she's done.

"What were you two talking about?" I ask Coach Marks after she's gone. "What did she say?"

His tone is cool. Chilly, even. "She says you need help."

84.

Then we're in the Markses' car, heading back to Alamo. The sun is shining on this Thanksgiving Day. Blue sky everywhere. California warmth and radiance.

I want to close my eyes but don't. My father died on this road seventeen years ago. He died scared and alone and not knowing his unborn son's fate. The worst sort of tragedy, but I've always loved him for caring enough to drop everything and come to where I was, to make sure I was okay, even when there was nothing he could've done to save me even if I'd needed saving. But today, for the first time ever, I'm glad he's gone. I'm glad he's not here to know me.

To see who I've become.

85.

Well, in addition to being an asshole who didn't bring medication home for his ailing mother, I'm also a coward, because when we get to the Markses' house and I see the broken window and the decorations for a Thanksgiving dinner that's gone cold and the small crowd of family waiting politely for our arrival while pretending they're doing normal things like watching football and playing Balderdash, I want to hide.

"I need to lie down," I say pitifully. Coach M nods and gestures for me to follow and leads me to a guest bedroom on the second floor that is wide and spacious and overlooks their lush backyard and glittering blue pool.

"This okay?" he asks, and how could a question like that not make me feel terrible after what I did? But he probably likes watching me squirm. I know I would if I were him.

I whisper that it's fine, but all the other things I long to say, like *I'm so, so sorry* and *Thank you* and *How can I make this right*, are wedged tight within me. They won't come out. I'm broken that way, I guess, although I don't know if that's a reason or an excuse.

Coach M also shows me where the bathroom is and what towels to use and where Winter will be staying—they've got a spare crib, courtesy of grandchildren who've since outgrown it, and it's as if my baby niece belongs here. As if she's always deserved better than me and my mother and the whole universe knows it. We return to the sunny bedroom and Coach M is still talking. He's telling me when they'll be eating and how I'm welcome to join them but that if I want to rest, they won't wake me up unless they hear something from my mother. This is code, I think: *Stay the fuck in your room and let us be.* Well, I can do that. So I nod obediently and then Coach Marks just stands there looking at me, with this mopey sort of expression, and hell if I know what he sees.

"I'm sorry about your mother," he says.

I grunt in response.

"You were the one who found her?"

I look away, my gaze returning to the window, to the warmth outside and the sparkling pool below. Anywhere but here. My knees feel weak and my head throbs, a strange rhythmic pounding as I focus on watching the sunlight dance along the water's surface. What Coach M is asking isn't something I want to talk about. It's not something I want to remember, either.

Coach Marks says something else. Something about tomorrow and where he'll be taking me and how he thinks it'll be for the best.

"Wait, what?" I ask. "What did you say?"

"Just sleep, Gus," he says. "Okay? And don't . . . don't worry about last night right now. I'm glad you're safe. That's what's important. I'll see you in the morning."

86.

The door closes behind him and I do what he says. Or at least I try. I lie down. Close my eyes. But sleep is elusive. For as much as I rail on the failures of others, I've never been immune to my own, and they come to gnaw at me, chewing at my conscience, my sense of sanity. Last night replays in my head—every moment—not just neglecting my mom, but stalking Lainey and being a creep at the party; trying to talk to Vince in the hallway and having him ignore me while that girl was hitting on him; running from Lainey the moment she found me when being with her was the first time in six months that I felt good. Not to mention everything I did by coming *here*. I destroyed my future. I know that. Coach M will never work with me again and I don't blame him. He barely wanted to work with me in the first place.

My actions were all self-sabotage. I realize this, although realizations are useless when they happen *after* you've fucked up. The only thing they're good for then is misery. Self-pity, too, which is just another mechanism of defeat. Only I'm not like Danny. I don't give up when I'm down.

I can't.

Sleep comes hours later, as the day dies, lured in by the warmth of laughter and conversation slipping through the floorboards beneath me. Regardless, my dreams are all nightmares. Tinged with guilt and laced with longing. There's horror there, too, in images I can't bear to see but did and always will.

This is what it means to be haunted. To remember, over and over, exactly what it is you wish to forget. To know that your worst moments will stay with you.

Define you.

No matter what.

87.

My eyes fly open to darkness. I gasp, limbs thrashing, and sweat soaks the sheets wrapped around me. I'm in a bed but it's not my bed and there's this sound I hear but can't locate. It crashes through my soul, again and again, a thundering drumbeat of dread.

Throwing off the covers, I sit up. Swing my legs to the floor. Moonlight fills the room with a cool blue glow and I have to be dreaming. This isn't my life I've woken to. It can't be. None of this is what I wanted. None of this is who I am.

On trembling legs, I crouch on the window seat and stare out at a strange world. A place I don't belong. All starlight and shadow. The clock on the nightstand tells me it's three a.m., and my heart whispers the truth.

I found her.

Followed by

It's all my fault.

I abandon the bedroom and make my way downstairs through a house that's dark. Silent. I know I'm in Coach M's place—the house I walked into only hours earlier. But nothing looks familiar. There are walls where there should be doors and rooms I don't recognize.

My stomach's hollow and I roam this foreign land, discovering first a living room, a dining room, then finally a massive kitchen with stone countertops and a greenhouse window filled with plants. Opening the refrigerator's French doors, I find that it's packed with Thanksgiving leftovers. Plates and Tupperware containers filled with turkey. Stuffing. Potatoes. Gravy. Pie of all kinds. I grab what I can, dumping it on the counter and stuffing my face. My fingers grow greasy, my stomach swells, but I keep eating until I gag on fresh cranberries, which are tarter than I'm prepared for.

I put back what's left but need something to wash it down. Back to the fridge, where open bottles of wine call to me. I pick something white and sweet that goes down easy. Then I finish off a bottle of merlot and that's plenty, I tell myself. I don't need to get sloppy or stupid. Not again. I take my time cleaning up, carefully stacking the empties in the recycling bin beneath the farmhouse sink and trying not to make a shit ton of noise while I'm at it.

When I'm done, the silence overwhelms me. There's only one answer, really, and its call grows greater the longer I stand in that kitchen. Or my resistance grows weaker. Either way, I end up outside, in the yard, by that sparkling pool, wearing nothing but my boxers. My feet sting, raw from the previous night's punishment of diving off the blocks. Standing in the damp grass is salt-in-the-wound agony, but sacrifice is all I know.

My intent is not training. I just want to wake up. I just want to find my way back to the life I knew.

Unlike last night, I don't dive. Instead I bend my aching muscles and bruised flesh to sit my ass on the pool deck. Then I dunk my sore feet below the surface and stare down my options. This body of water is neither deep nor wide.

But it's here. And it'll do.

I slip in.

I slide under.

88.

Lainey wasn't the breaking point between Danny and me. I can't pretend this was the case any more than I can pretend Lainey wasn't aware of the raging crush I had on her. But by that point I already loathed Danny, and I loathed myself more for not seeing through his dumb act earlier than I did. But it broke my heart when he broke hers, in part because she wouldn't be coming around our house any longer. But hurting someone as kind and giving as Lainey was a dick move. So rather than sulk alone the way I always did, I went to Danny and told him what I thought of him. Right to his face.

I'd never seen my brother so mad. His face clouded with fury. He leapt to his feet. Advanced toward me until I felt his breath on my cheek.

"What did you say?" he snapped.

I burned with fury. "I said you're an asshole. You don't deserve a girl like Lainey. You don't deserve anything."

He shoved me and he kept shoving, driving me into the wall of his bedroom and using his arm to pin me back with such force I could scarcely breathe. "I don't want to hear her goddamn name come of out of your fucking mouth ever again."

"Lainey," I shot back. "And you're the one who fucked her. Not me."

Danny laughed, releasing his hold. "So that's what this is about? You're jealous of me and you want to fuck my girl? Is that the reason you're always sniffing after her when she's over here? You just want to take everything I have, don't you? Just like everybody else. You can't do anything for yourself and now you want to rip me open and scavenge me for parts."

I snorted. "You wish."

"Shut up."

"You're crazy," I told him. "You're fucking paranoid if you think I want to be anything like you."

Danny shoved me again. Harder this time, so that my head slammed the wall with a bang. I saw stars but shoved him back with a snarl. Then I did it. I put my shoulder down and charged, knocking Danny off-balance before I reared back and took a swing. My fist to his jaw.

It landed.

Danny fell back with a yelp, his fingers grasping for the spot on his chin where I'd struck him. I stood, tensed, ready for more, but he just stared at me with his mouth wide open, seemingly realizing for the first time how much I had grown. At fourteen, I wasn't a child anymore. In fact, I was only a few inches shorter than Danny, and I'd be stronger than him someday. I was sure of it.

"Stay the fuck away from me," he growled.

"Or what?"

"You don't want to find out."

Now it was my turn to laugh. His words were an empty threat and for once, we both knew it. I turned and walked from his room feeling better about myself than I had in years. This lasted roughly a week, when I found out he was back with Lainey again. But at least he made an effort to stay out of my way. That is, until one night, six months later, when I woke to find him in my room, hovering over my bed like a ghost.

"What do you want?" I tried rolling away from him. The air in my room was hot and miserable.

"I need to talk to you." Danny shook my leg. "Wake the fuck up."

"Go *away*."

He shook harder. "Did you hear what I said?"

"Fine." I rolled over to look at him. The hall light backlit

Danny's shape and distorted his features so that he resembled an alien trying to make contact. I sat up and switched on my desk lamp, squinting to get a better look. My brother was seventeen, still two years away from death, but the expression on his face was an eerie omen of what was to come. Danny didn't look like Danny. His eyes were bloodshot, puffy, his skin oily and pale.

"What's wrong?" I asked.

"Can you keep a secret?" He pushed his hair back, sat on the chair next to me, and swung his legs around. My nose wrinkled. Something about him *reeked*. Usually meticulous about his grooming and his looks, Danny smelled like he hadn't showered in days.

"Why *me*?" I squeaked.

"Because I need your help."

"What kind of help?"

"I want you to keep these for me." Danny shoved something into my hand. A plastic Ziploc bag filled with pill bottles. "Put them somewhere where I can't find them."

"What're they?" Thoughts of Darien flitted through my mind. I held the bottles under the incandescent bulb and strained to read the prescription labels. Relief rushed through me. They were Klonopin, Ambien, and Prozac, all pills he'd been prescribed for his anxiety and insomnia. The labels on the bottles had dire warnings about not mixing the medication with alcohol or anything else sedating.

"Don't they work?" I asked.

"Yeah. Sure, they work, I guess."

"Does that mean you're sleeping better?"

"Not at all."

"Then why do you want me to have them?"

"I don't want them near me. They make me feel . . ." Danny twitched, shuddered. Clawed at his own throat.

"They make you feel what?"

"Scared," he whispered.

I said nothing. I didn't understand what Danny had to be

scared of. He had everything—the girl, the coach, the future of unlimited potential. He had everything I wanted, but in a sick way I admired his refusal to take pills for something that to me seemed like a matter of mental toughness. That meant he was strong and capable, not weak like Darien, who took any shortcut to numb her pain. Danny might be an asshole, but at least he had conviction.

So I accepted the pills, waved him off, and kept them buried somewhere in my room. Danny never mentioned that night again, and I didn't either because with whatever crisis he was facing averted, he went right back to swimming. Right back to winning. Right back to treating me like the whipping boy he saw me as. In fact, he grew more insufferable than he'd been before the fight we'd had over Lainey. I didn't understand it. I'd done him a favor and now it was like he was going out of his way to make me miserable. No, I couldn't practice driving in his car. No, I couldn't get a ride to my meet. Yes, I could sit and talk with his girlfriend while he made her wait downstairs, but later he'd tell her about the time I shit my pants after getting food poisoning from a breakfast burrito at Jack in the Box.

But now, as I glide through the water of his coach's pool, I can't help but wonder why he gave those pills to me and what he thought I might do with them. In hindsight, it's not hard to imagine what his fears were. It's not hard to understand who he was afraid of and why he felt so unsafe. But maybe he thought I'd tell someone about the pills. Or that he could provoke me into telling. Maybe he trusted that I would do *something* and I didn't, and that's why he did what he did in the way that he did it.

Or maybe . . . he didn't think about me at all.

89.

I leave a note before I go.

It's not one I've personally written; no, it's Danny's envelope for Coach Marks that I should have given up long ago and that I find crumpled in my jacket pocket from last night. Keeping it all this time was a shitty thing to do. I know that now and I know I've never been the one that matters. All this chasing after my brother's legacy has only proved what my mother was trying to tell me in the first place: I don't know how to create one of my own.

Who in their right mind envies the dead?

90

My hair wet, my body shivering from the cold, I walk away from Coach M's house. It takes a lot to push aside my guilt for abandoning Winter, but she'll be loved here. Cared for. Far better than what I could give her, so I hit the road—on foot; I don't have a car out here—in the grainy haze of predawn darkness and make my way toward the highway that will lead me to my mother, which is where I need to go. I failed Danny, and my father, and I failed her, too. The least I can do is apologize.

The least I can do is be better than who I am.

The walk's endless. A winding maze of empty streets, expensive cars, sleeping strip malls lined with day spas and restaurants adorned with uninspired names like *Gentle Greens* or *Vitality Bowls*, which make it sound like the most important thing about their food is that it'll pass successfully through your digestive tract.

I reach the highway, at last. Five lanes of tractor exhaust and roadkill turn my stomach, but I take the shoulder heading north. I stick my thumb out a couple times but it's wasted effort. There's not enough daylight and not enough traffic. Black Friday's sleeping late or moved online or who the fuck knows. What I do know is that my mom's at John Muir Hospital, which is up in Walnut Creek, a good eight miles away. It's also where I was born and where my mom was when she got the news my father had died. Right on this very road. I don't know the exact spot where he lost his life, but it can't be far.

My clothes are dark; I hang close to the guardrail, my shoes stumbling over gravel and broken glass. Trucks and cars blow past me, their wheels throwing up chunks of dust, dirt, and fumes. I cough, choke. My eyes sting. A couple of the trucks honk and shout, but no one stops. My head hurts, my feet ache. I keep going.

I pass housing developments, fast-food restaurants, then a long stretch of ranch land. Horses linger in dewy grass, heads lowered, tails flicking flies, and the sun is beginning to peek over the mountain—bright bursts of golden rays like the hand of God itself is reaching down to touch the animals. I stop to watch. To breathe in the scent of wet grass and truck exhaust. It's strange, the way nature's cordoned off by man-made choices. But boundaries exist for a reason, and this is when I see it. On the hillside, maybe a hundred yards away, beneath the widespread branches of a giant oak tree, a mare and her foal struggle desperately, trapped by something that's hidden in shadows.

Clambering up the roadway, I find the fence lined with razor wire but climb it anyway. My arms are scratched, bleeding, my clothes torn, but I make it to the other side. I slip running up the hill, sliding on dew and long grass, but I get up, over and over, until I reach the oak tree where I can see that the foal's hindquarters are pinned beneath a fallen branch. The injuries are bad from what I can tell, and the mare is frantic. I tug at the branch but can't lift it on my own, so I turn and run farther up the hill toward the darkened ranch house. A yellow dog barks as I draw closer but I spot people in the barn, four men in jeans, flannel, throwing flakes of hay onto the bed of a truck and I shout to them and wave my arms, calling out that there's an animal hurt, a baby that needs help.

The men stop to look at me but don't make a move to follow me at all, to go where I'm pointing.

"I need your help!" I cry.

They still don't move.

"An animal's hurt! One of the babies."

"No baby," one of the men says.

"What?"

"I said there are no babies in the field."

"But I saw it!"

He shakes his head and I reach for his arm, to bring him with me, but he steps back, holds me off. I lunge again and he shoves me. Furious, I swing back. The other guys are on me in an instant, shouting at me to calm down, pulling me back. I'm thrown to the ground. My head hits dirt, ringing my ears and blurring my vision.

Fuck this. Fuck everyone. I stagger to my feet and flip them off before turning to head back toward the horses. I'll figure something out if they won't, although my head is in agony and even though the sun's starting to rise, it's growing harder for me to see. I stumble through the grass, following my footsteps, but I can't find the oak tree and the stuck foal. I keep looking but my legs burn from the running and the falling and the torment I put them through the previous night. A thundering of hooves and a fresh swell of dust freeze me in place as the horses stampede up the hill, heading for the silhouetted flatbed truck rumbling along the ridgeline while the men throw hay into the grass.

I'm better off leaving. The pinned foal must be fine and if it's not, it'll suffer and die because everything suffers and dies, and I can't remember why I cared about the animal to start with. I crawl back over razor wire to the highway shoulder and my stomach's bleeding, which means I'll probably need a tetanus shot to avoid lockjaw, but I'm on my original path again. I'm walking toward where my father was killed and where my own life ended in any practical sense of the word, since I was the one who sent my mother to the hospital in the first place and this is why she'll never love me.

My ankle buckles. A bright shot of pain. I limp forward as the sun grows brighter, but it's hard to know if I'm here or if I'm there, on that shining spring day when my brother died and left me alone to find him on my own. I came home from school that afternoon and pounded up the stairs. I didn't know he was coming home, but Danny had put music on and he knew my schedule and that I'd be the one to get there first.

He knew what I would see.

Finding my brother felt like Danny's punishment for me. I was alone, all alone, and I had to cut him down and call for help and try to breathe life back into his cold, vomit-specked lips. He'd made pasta in the kitchen before hanging himself and I could taste the sauce with each desperate rescue breath the 911 operator told me to force into his lungs. My nostrils were filled with the stench of tomatoes and bile and worse. And all of it, everything about that day, felt like vengeance. Or retribution. That even in death Danny would ensure my misery.

It made sense. I'd taken his father and so Danny took everything he could from me. I guess I hate him for that—I hate him for a lot of things—but the truth is that I'll always hate myself more. If our father meant that much to Danny and my mother, he must've been someone special. He must've been worth grieving—he must have been a better person than I am.

Unloosed, unmoored, the rest of my memories of the day Danny died fly free, buzzing from my head in a vicious swarm. Like raptors after prey, they claw at my consciousness and threaten to swallow me whole. I'm consumed by an assault on my senses—a wicked cacophony of flashing lights and blaring sirens. Penance, I think. This is penance for my sins. I killed my father, which killed Danny, and I almost killed my mother, too. Even Winter hasn't escaped my grip unscathed.

I grab my head with both hands, but the pain's unbearable. Everything hurts, only I can't pinpoint where it's coming from. The noise swells louder and I look over my shoulder, and that's when I actually *see* the noise. It's floating behind me and coming closer, muddled in the spinning blue and red lights of a cop car. An ambulance, too. But I'm not in our house or Danny's room on the second floor, so I sit down hard on the highway shoulder and lift my arms and wave for them to come to me because at this point, even if I haven't technically given up, my life is over.

You know, there's not much to say about being picked up by the cops on the side of the road and getting hauled off to juvie for trespassing and attempted assault. But it really sucks. I can tell you that much.

92.

The next few days are a blur. I'm transferred out of Alameda County, back to Contra Costa, where I'm held in a juvenile facility until Monday. This is when I'm released into my mother's care, although it's not clear to me whether that's because of the holiday weekend or the fact that she's been in the hospital. Either way, she shows up right on time and I wrap my arms around her before I have a chance to think better of it. I don't really know what else to do.

"I was so scared," I tell her.

"Shh," she says.

"I'm sorry. I'm so, so sorry."

"I am, too." She sighs heavily and presses her chin to my chest.

A surge of panic hits me. "Where's Winter?"

"At home. Cleo's watching her. She's excited to see you."

We meet with my caseworker, who says she won't recommend filing charges against me, seeing as I was the only one who was hurt and that I've never been in trouble before and anyway, the men at the horse farm just wanted to make sure I was okay. This is a relief, obviously, but then she has to tell my mother that they came this close to putting me on a psych hold because of my erratic actions and inability to care for myself. It's beyond embarrassing, hearing this, but I get stupid about it and start crying, which really only proves her point. My mother pats my shoulder and thanks the woman for her concern because what else can she do?

After that, I'm set free.

We head for home.

"I think I do need help," I tell my mom in the car on the ride home. My teeth chatter and my hands are shaking. "I don't know what's happening to me. I'm losing my fucking mind."

"It's okay, Gus," she says. "We'll figure it out."

"We will?"

My mother nods, navigating her way through a left-turn-light cycle at the very last moment before she turns to look at me. "Absolutely. Everything will be fine. You will be fine. I promise you that. Okay?"

Well, I know enough about life and death and black swan theory to know that no one can promise me the future, but hearing her say this is enough to reassure me, which is maybe the same thing. Either way, basking in the warmth of her words and the comfort they provide, I'm finally able to lean back, draw my legs beneath me, and sleep.

94.

"How old are you?" I ask Marco when we meet in his office the following week for our first one-on-one therapy session together.

"Is that important for you to know?" He's sitting across from me, looking flustered in the exact way I remember him looking, and I really shouldn't give him shit about his age. Not when I'm the one who called and begged for him to see me, after he'd tried giving my mother a referral to a more experienced clinician. He agreed, finally, after speaking with his supervisor, and I'm authorized to see him twice a week. Apparently, I meet medical necessity now, so in addition to therapy, I've got a psychiatrist who's keeping me dutifully sedated while the mood stabilizer and antidepressant she's prescribed take hold. The end result has been a lot of sleeping. Too much, really. The only time I've left the house for anything other than medical appointments was to send an apology to Coach Marks and his wife, along with payment for their window, and I slept on the couch for six hours after walking to the mailbox.

"It's not important," I tell Marco. "How old you are. I was just wondering. You seem really young."

His shoulders relax. "I *am* young. Sorry to be defensive about it. I get a lot of parents asking if I have kids of my own, which I don't, and then I have to prove to them that I know anything at all about working with teens."

"Well, that sucks," I say.

"Just part of the job." He looks at me. "How're you doing?"

"Can't be all that good if I'm sitting here."

"I've heard."

"Yeah."

"How are you adjusting to the medication?"

"I don't know. I kind of feel like puking a lot, but Dr. S says that'll go away."

"Did she give you anything for the nausea?"

"It's not helping."

"Have you been losing weight?"

"About ten pounds."

Marco writes something on a piece of paper. "That's concerning."

"It's not all from the meds, though. It's just sort of hard for me to do anything these days. That includes eating."

"Sounds like the depression's pretty bad right now."

I nod and close my eyes. Wish I were anywhere but here.

"I'm sorry, Gus," he says. "I know this is hard."

I shrug. Therapists sure do like pointing out the obvious.

"My primary concern today is with keeping you safe. It worries me that you're not able to stay nourished. And it worries me to see you in so much pain."

"Oh," I say.

"I want to ensure you're getting the care you need. In the immediate future as well as longer term. Finding a loved one who's died by suicide has lasting effects. That was a real trauma, and it makes sense that you're still dealing with it."

I open my eyes again. "You think I'm going to kill myself?"

"That's not what I said."

"It's what everyone thinks. But that would be selfish, wouldn't it? Doing what Danny already did."

Marco frowns. "Do you worry a lot about being selfish? Or being like your brother?"

"Not really. Well, maybe the brother part."

"Do you want to kill yourself?"

"No," I say slowly. "I don't think so."

"Have you ever tried to hurt yourself? In any way?"

"Not in a long time."

"When?"

I pull my sleeves up to show him the scars.

"What're those?" he asks.

"They're from sixth grade. I mean, I wasn't trying to die or anything. I was just having a hard time. My sister was using a lot at the time. She overdosed twice. It was really shitty."

"I'm sure it was," Marco says. "What does your coach think about those scars?"

"I don't know. It's not something I talk about with him. It was a long time ago."

"Maybe we should talk about it."

"I guess. I don't feel very good right now, though."

"Another time, then."

"Sure."

Marco leans forward. "Did you ever read that note I wrote to you? On the last day of group?"

I think back. "No."

"Did you read any of the messages the other group members wrote to you?"

I shake my head. "I'm sorry. I'm really sorry."

"You don't have to be sorry, Gus. I told you to choose when you read them. But if you don't mind the nudge, I'd suggest you read those notes sooner rather than later."

I call Lainey on Christmas Eve. It's not a good idea but I do it anyway, and there's no way to spin my actions as anything less than selfishness.

So I guess I am like Danny. In some ways.

"Hey," she says softly. "How are you?"

"I'm okay. A little, you know, stressed or something."

"I think the holidays are always hard when you've lost someone."

I lost you, I want to say. "How's school?"

"We're on break, but I love it up here. It's snowing, you know. I can see it gathering on the windowsill."

"You're there right now?"

"Yeah. I have a job. Couldn't make it back for Christmas this year. And . . ."

"And what?"

"It's nice being away. In my own place. Doing my own thing. The job's mostly an excuse to get a break from my family and all the shit that comes from being around them. They're a lot. It's a good feeling, you know—figuring out who the hell you are on your own. Without all that baggage."

"That hasn't happened for me yet."

"It will."

"Your sister hates me, by the way."

Lainey laughs. "Don't let it go to your head. You're not the only one."

"Hey, what did you end up studying?"

"International finance. They've got a great program up here and I've got an internship lined up in Chicago next summer. I might study in France next fall."

"I'm really sorry," I blurt out. "About what happened at that party last month. I wanted to tell you that."

"Oh," Lainey says. "It's okay. It really—it wasn't a big deal. I was just worried about you."

"It's *not* okay."

"I'm telling you it is."

"I fucked up a lot that night. Not just with you. Other shit, too."

"What'd you fuck up?"

"Let's see, I threw a rock at Coach M's house. Broke a window and yelled at him while I was drunk."

"Oh wow, that's classy."

"And I almost killed my mom."

"Literally or figuratively?"

"Literally."

Her tone grows serious. "Shit. Is she okay?"

"She's fine."

"I think your mom hates me even more than my sister hates you."

"She does?"

"You didn't know that? I don't think I was good enough for her Danny."

"I don't think anyone was."

"That's true. Well, what else did you fuck up?"

"Winter . . ." I say as my voice finally cracks. "She could've been hurt, L. Because of me."

"Oh, Gus," she says.

"What do I do? How can I make any of this better?"

"I don't know. I think you just have to find a way to move forward. To make amends. And do better."

"I miss you, Lainey," I say helplessly. "I really, really do."

She pauses. "You're feeling sad tonight, aren't you? Is that why you called?"

"Yes," I whisper.

"I get sad sometimes, too. You want to know what helps me feel better?"

"What's that?" I ask.

And she tells me.

97.

Lainey's advice is to face a fear, but I don't actually get up the nerve to do this until the Monday after New Year's, when I haul my ass to the club for 5:30 a.m. practice. Hell, I'd be lying if I said I wasn't self-conscious. Thanks to Zoloft and my recent lack of physical activity, I've gained back the ten pounds I lost, but not in a good way. My body feels soft and woefully out of shape. But I'm here, so I should probably revise one of my rules of greatness. Rather than *Don't ever let anyone tell you what you can't do*, I think it should be *Keep listening. Some truths are worth hearing.*

When I get there, Fitz and Vince are the only other guys in the locker room. My head hurts and I can feel them staring at me, but I get down to the business of changing, the motions of my routine.

"Hey, Gus," Vince says easily. "You doing okay, man?"

"Yeah."

"Happy New Year."

"Happy New Year," I say.

"Where've you been?"

"Coach didn't tell you?"

Vince shrugs. "Nah."

"I've been sick."

"Sick?"

"Yeah."

"You missed *Vancouver*."

"I know."

Fitz frowns. "Does that mean you're better now?"

"I don't know."

"You sure you should be swimming?"

"I'm sure it's not any of your fucking business."

Vince laughs. Loudly. "There's our Gus. Good to have you back."

Then it's time for practice. My stomach's filled with storm clouds, keeping me in the changing room longer than I intend, but it's not like I can back out now. I stand by the sink. Catch my breath. And when I know I won't vomit, I go for it. I grab my towel, my goggles, my swim cap, and head out toward the pool.

This may not be greatness—not even close—but it's a start.

98.

Fitz and Vince are already in the water by the time I get out there. Even so, I know they're watching me. Hell, I'd watch me, too.

Steam rises off the water to mingle with the mist, as I walk toward where Coach Marks is standing on the pool deck. He's wrapped in a thick coat, a hint of stubble dots his chin, but he's the same person he's always been. The one who watched my brother fall.

The one who tried to catch me.

"Hey," I say.

Coach M turns to look at me.

"I'm here to swim. I mean, if that's okay?"

He doesn't say anything, just continues to look at my face, and I don't know what he's seeing. The kid he hates or the one he loved.

"I've got a shrink now," I tell him. "I go every week. And I'm taking medication. Antidepressants. A mood stabilizer. It's all helping. But I . . ."

"But what?"

"I need to be here. Please. Nothing's changed about that."

He nods.

"So this is okay?"

"You said you needed to be here. I guess it'll have to be, right?"

"You aren't mad at me?"

"Does that matter?"

"I don't know," I say.

He sighs heavily. "Me either. But get in. We'll figure it out together."

99.

I turn and dive.

The cold hits me first. It's a shock, a full-body assault that jolts me to my core and claws for every nerve ending. The pressure hits next, all weight and constriction, squeezing down on my lungs, my throat.

The space between my bones.

It hurts, but my muscles know what to do, how to push me forward, and as I begin to move beneath the surface in a sleek undulating rhythm, I quickly find the pleasure in the pain. *This* is what I've wanted. What I've craved. It was never the drowning or the danger or the darkness pooling in the fathoms beneath me. Like the shark that needs oxygen running through its gills, I've always needed this fluid quickening, this aquatic shock and awe. To swim is to fly—an earthly scrap of magic.

It's a miracle, really.

I work the practice diligently. Coach Marks won't tell me my times or anything, but I'm winded quickly, which is all the data I need. My goals may not have changed but the challenge has.

"It'll be like coming back from any illness or injury," Coach Marks assures me when we're done. "It takes more discipline and mental strength to know when to hold back than it does to push, but all that means is that the future is yours if you want it. It's in your control."

"Wasn't it always in my control?"

He furrows his brow. "I don't know. Not everything is."

"Well, I guess I'll see you tonight, then."

"I'll be here," he says.

"Are you surprised I'm back?"

"A little."

"Do you think we'll be okay?" I ask.

"Who?"

"You and me, I guess. I want to make up for everything I did. I'm talking to the club director later about making up for breaking into the pool. Doing community service or working to pay off any damage. But with you—"

"We'll work on it," he says.

"You still think I can make the Trials?"

"You still think I have answers?"

"I guess not."

"That's still what you want, though?"

"Yeah."

"Why?"

I bite my lip and shake my head. It's not that I don't know the answer. I just don't know how to say it.

He sighs. "When you figure it out, let me know, okay?"

"Sure."

"In your control means exactly that. I won't stop you, whatever it is you want to do. Not unless . . ."

"Unless what?"

The look he gives me is a pointed one. "I think you know."

I nod.

"Now go home, Gus," he says.

So I do.

100.

Healing is an active verb. This is what Marco tells me over the next few weeks, whenever we meet. Most of the time I think he's full of shit, but he's probably right about this. Forgiveness isn't a light switch or a magic wand. It's work.

This is also what it feels like being under Coach M's guidance again, and I don't even mean the swimming part. Getting him to believe in me again is also an active process, although to me it seems as if he's determined to be passive when it comes to my training. We're not fighting, but we're also not *doing* anything, not as partners, and that feels wrong.

"It feels wrong not to fight?" Marco asks.

"No. It feels wrong that he doesn't care enough to fight."

"You have an interesting way of interpreting care."

I flop back on the chair. "Yeah, I get that. But he pushes all his top swimmers. It's what he does and what he's supposed to do and he's not doing it with me."

"Then it sounds like he needs more time."

"It's been six weeks! I've been doing everything he asks of me. Training just how he wants me to and not being an asshole like I used to be."

"And?"

"And it's working. Somewhat. My times are going down. I feel strong when I'm in the water. Stronger than ever, really."

"So what's the problem?"

"*He's* the problem! It's how he looks at me. How he treats me.

He's still pissed about what I did at his house that night and I understand that. But why's he working with me if he hates me? Why would he do that?"

Marco appears nonplussed. "Maybe he doesn't hate you?"

"It sure feels like he does."

"That's not the same thing."

"I *know* that. Why don't you just tell me how to fix it."

"I don't know how to fix your relationship with your coach. Your guess is as good as mine. Better even, if you think about it."

I throw my hands up. I mean, this is the problem with talking about your feelings, isn't it? Nothing ever changes. Insight isn't an answer. It's just bullshit masquerading as more.

"What're you thinking about, Gus?" Marco asks.

"Honestly?"

"Yes, honestly."

"I'm thinking about how much you suck at what you get paid to do," I say.

But Marco just laughs. "See, there's that wisdom of yours."

101

"Wake up, Bennett," Coach M barks at me the next morning. The sky's overcast, swiped with a gloomy coat of gray, and I'm the first one in the water. A blissful emergence: steam sweeps across the surface like dragon's breath.

"I *am* awake," I call back.

"Doesn't look like it."

"Just warming up."

"Well, warm faster," he snipes before walking off in a huff.

I flutter-kick forward in response. I don't know what's up his ass today. Okay, actually, I do know what's up his ass because I saw him drop hot coffee all over the ground and his shoes while he was walking from the parking lot. Sucks for him, but whatever. I got here early for a reason.

Breathing deep, I dip beneath the surface to touch the bottom of the pool. My ears pop, and the world around me closes in fast, but rather than focus on the fact that I'm slowly drowning, I simply let myself be. It's strange what I notice when I'm not in motion, when I'm not trying to get to the other side. The water's squeezing me, but my body holds strong, and this is a natural truth, I guess; everything comes down to displacement and occupation.

Give and take.

Grief bubbles inside me, a low rumbling of pain. Of remorse. Being this deep reminds me of the night I fell into the diving pool and had to find my way out. It also reminds me of Danny, who didn't.

It's an odd sensation: these sharp moments of sadness that I have for Danny. They're new and growing more frequent, and Marco says I should just let these moments be. That I should acknowledge their presence and accept them for what they are and that allowing myself to have any kind of emotion other than anger is progress.

Eventually my lungs protest and I begin to float upward and kick. Not hard. Not fast. Once my head emerges, I ease into my stroke and pull my body through the smooth water with nothing but weightlessness in my mind.

Soon the others join me in the water and when everyone's warmed up and loose, we get out again and shiver on the deck while Coach Marks outlines the workout.

"It's going to be intervals today, boys," he says. "Progressive. I hope you're ready."

"Fucking hell," mutters Vince, because progressive workouts are legendary for how shitty they are.

Coach M glares in response. "Let's make it doubles, then."

"Nice going, Vince," Fitz grumbles.

The coach starts clapping. "Let's go. Let's go. Let's go."

We step up to our lanes.

"Well, he's kind of a major asshole today, isn't he?" Vince whispers at the exact moment Coach M blows his whistle.

I laugh in spite of myself, which means my start is late. I hit the water a good half second behind the rest of the guys, but I don't let it get to me. I shake it off and go for it. But rather than my normal drumbeat push of "faster, motherfucker," I keep my muscles loose and easy, and focus on maintaining an image of my body as less of a bulldozing force than pure grace. I'm not fighting the pool.

I'm part of it.

<hr />

It's the end of practice and Coach Marks is walking toward me. I'm wary. He's still got that gloomy rain cloud look hanging over his head, but I swear to myself that I'm not going to get into anything with him. It's not productive. It's not going to help me.

"Hey, Coach," I say.

"How'd that feel?" he asks.

"Pretty good, I guess."

"It was better than good."

"Really?" I stare up at him. Bite my tongue. He's the one with the stopwatch. The knowledge.

He nods tersely, but there's a gleam in his eye. Spilled coffee and all. He's *excited*, I realize.

About me.

"How good?" I ask carefully.

"Good enough that I think you should be racing again. If your mom agrees."

My heart pounds. "She will. I know she will."

He grunts. "There's a meet in Kansas City. Second week of March. You qualify there, you make the Trials in Omaha with ten weeks to spare. It's . . . it'll be close. But it's what you want, am I right?"

Is this happening? "Yes. Absolutely."

"Good."

"Do you think I have a shot?"

"I wouldn't send you if I didn't."

"That's not an answer."

Coach Marks is silent for a moment, no doubt sparing my feelings, but what I want is for him to be honest. To tell me what he thinks of me and if he has faith in my character as well as my ability. What he says instead is: "Epic, huh?"

"What?"

"That was the word you used that night you came to my house. It's what you said you wanted to be."

My cheeks warm. "It's something Danny used to say."

"Well, it's my word. Not Danny's. He learned it from me."

"Okay."

Coach M shakes his head. Scratches his chin. "I just thought you should know that."

102.

In early March, Fitz is offered spots at USC, UC Berkeley, and the University of Texas at Austin.

"Stanford didn't want you?" I tease.

He grins. "Maybe I didn't want them."

"What's your top choice?"

"Berkeley would be easy," he says with a sigh. "That's where my folks want me to go. Keep me close and everything."

"Would you still swim here?"

"I don't know." He looks at me. "Why did Danny leave the club? He could've stayed on. I was sure he would."

I shrug. I'd been sure of it, too. It's what my mom had wanted for him and it led to the biggest fight I ever saw between them. He'd made her *cry*, telling her she was lucky he was bothering to stick around in California in the first place. That he'd leave for good if she didn't stop bitching about what she wanted and start caring about his needs. I don't know. I understood what he was saying— that guilt wasn't the reason he wanted to choose a school—but he was so *mean* about it. Maybe, if I'd been a good son, I would've stood up for my mother in that moment. Or maybe I should've taken Danny's side. In the end, I didn't take either. Instead I watched them tear into each other with the same glee with which I'd watched the new Godzilla flick. *Let them fight.*

But now I say: "Danny must've thought he'd do better in LA. Or maybe he felt he owed them his loyalty for picking him."

"Loyalty," Fitz echoes.

"Yeah."

"That's a complicated idea."

"Is it?"

"Definitely. I mean, Coach M probably told him it was okay to go. That he should follow his heart or something."

"Yeah, maybe."

Fitz looks at me. "See, I really hate these kinds of choices. When the answer isn't obvious and all this subtext is floating beneath the waterline. On the one hand, do I want him to beg me to stay and feel needed? Like I'm someone worth fighting for? Or do I want him to tell me to go so that it doesn't hurt when I actually leave?"

"Well, what do *you* want?"

"Everything."

I smile. "Good luck with that."

"What about you?" Fitz asks. "What would you do?"

"No fucking clue," I say, but I don't imagine it would be difficult for me to leave. Not when I already feel unwanted. But when I think about my father and what it must've meant to Danny to lose him at such a young age, I can also imagine that Coach M telling him to go might've felt less like independence and more like abandonment. To Danny, it was probably a betrayal, even if it was what he wanted to do anyway, which is the really screwed-up part. But that's the thing about tragedy. By definition, there's no winning.

Only loss.

103.

"You nervous?" Coach M asks me on the plane ride out to Kansas City. We both know this meet represents both hope and failure. It's my first and last shot to do what I should've done last year in Vancouver.

"Not at all," I say coolly.

"Good."

Silence hangs between us—this is a strange trip, just me and him. Fitz is off to Austin soon and Vince isn't on the national circuit level yet. He's still developing. Still taking his time, which is a good thing. He'll get there. But I don't know. I thought I would feel proud in this moment, the victor gilded with spoils, but it's not like that at all. There's something apocalyptic about being the last one standing. About continuing to chase a dream that's already tried to take me down. Am I more or less prepared than I was back in November?

Am I a better or worse person?

The plane shakes, a sharp rattling that prompts the *fasten your seat belts* announcement. I set my jaw, grind my teeth. Try not to lose my shit until the ride smooths out.

"Therapy going okay?" Coach M asks.

My heart's still racing. I peek out at blue sky and tell myself nothing bad happens when the sun's shining. "You asking if I'm keeping up with it? I am. Every week. Taking my meds, too."

"Your guy any good?"

"I don't know," I say, although this answer is both a truth and a lie. I like Marco but I'm not sure he really gets me.

"Should find a new one if he's not."

"Yeah?"

"I mean it. It's like finding the right coach. Took me a while."

"To find a coach?"

"A therapist."

"You see a therapist?"

"Yeah. Less so now than when I was younger. But I went back after Danny for a while. It helped."

"Huh," I say.

"Does that surprise you?"

"I guess it does. Although my mom's seeing someone, too. And taking meds."

"Is that good?"

"So far."

"It's worth finding the right person. It's worth knowing what you want from the process, too." He pauses. "Actually, I made an appointment for next week. With the anniversary coming up and everything . . . well, it seemed like a good idea."

"Oh." The anniversary isn't a topic I'm willing to engage in, but now Coach Marks has got me wondering. Not about him and why he might need someone to talk to. But if he means more than he's saying. Should I be second-guessing my therapist?

Or should I be second-guessing *him*?

"Hey, can I ask you a question?" I say.

"Sure."

"Does anybody else . . . do they know what happened to me? Why I didn't swim in Vancouver and all?"

"I haven't told anybody anything. It's not my place."

"So what do they think?"

"Don't know," he says.

104.

Well, I don't know, either, and it's a question that gnaws at me, won't let me sleep at night. And the next morning, as I walk into the meet on weary bones, I know something's wrong. I recognize a lot of the other swimmers, the other coaches, but it's as if no one wants to make eye contact with me. They have to know something, or at least they think they do.

Like the fact that I'm a fraud.

And unstable.

And hell-bent on exploiting my brother's death for my own selfish means.

All three are true, but in my newfound state of trying to move toward healing, I didn't anticipate how this would affect me. It's like a knife's edge stabbing at my pride. I'm a fraud, aren't I? Less Ali than Danny, even, since everything I offered up about myself was a lie. But I'm here and I refuse to let anyone see my frailty, and besides, there's always bitterness to draw from.

So this is how I do it. Chin up. Shoulders back. I walk onto the pool deck and no one gives me a second look, but I'm as arrogant as always. A pure thoroughbred among a field of nags. The darkest horse.

I know what I came here to do.

And I do it.

Just barely.

The crowd cheers when my time goes up for the 400 m. They

love a winner and I did well for them, which means they're back on my side, willing to overlook my flaws. I glance over at Coach M, eager to see that gleam of pleasure in his eye.

But it's not there.

105.

No turbulence this time, but our flight home is equally awkward. This should be a festive moment, a touchpoint of shared celebration—and it is. But it also isn't.

It's not until we're in the car that I'm able to put words to my thoughts.

"You pissed that I qualified or that I didn't do better?"

"What?" he says.

"I'm better than my brother. My time proved it and that kills you, doesn't it? You didn't really want me to do it."

"That's not true."

"Then why are you so pissy with me?"

"Well, for starters, you could've done better."

"That's why you're mad?"

"Not exactly."

"Then why?"

"I'm worried about you," he says quietly. "Watching you today really scared me."

"Because of Danny?"

"Of *course* because of Danny. You've been swimming so beautifully these past few months. You stopped fighting me and yourself and you were working with the water, not against it. But today that wasn't there at all. You went all the way back to October. You fought the whole way."

"I just qualified for the Olympic Trials and you're critiquing my *style*?"

"I'm your coach."

"So what're you saying? That I'm not good enough? That you think I'm going to choke the way he did? That's really what I want to hear right now. Thanks a lot."

"No!" He hits the dash with the palm of his hand. "Gus, I'm not worried about you *choking*! That's the last fucking thing I'm thinking about."

"Then what?"

He stares at me, his jaw hanging open. "Jesus, kid. Are you seriously this dense?"

"I guess I am." I slide my earbuds in, turn my music on, and tune his bullshit out.

106.

"Holy shit," a voice says. "Would you look who it is."

This is a surprise. My sister, Darien, is standing in the front doorway when I arrive home. Coach M just dropped me off, and I'm running on no sleep, ready to crawl into bed, when I spot her. My first thought is that she's a mirage. A vision from the past. But her form doesn't waver and when she sees me, she waves and smiles like it's no big deal before stepping all the way outside to bask in the early-spring warmth with Winter perched on her hip.

I stop short. Any remaining glow of positivity from the meet rushes out of me. This is bad. I know for a fact this isn't the start of a redemption arc. Darien, who leaves and returns, again and again, is—and always will be—the prodigal child. Also, she looks like shit.

"What're you doing here?" I ask, although I fear it's obvious. At my urging and the advice of our family's social worker, my mom's been working with a lawyer to get legal custody of Winter. The importance of this grew clear after what happened in November with CFS, who asked a lot of questions about why Winter was living with us and not her legal guardian. As far as I know, Darien hasn't responded to any of the phone calls or messages the lawyer's left for her, but that's no surprise. She also hasn't asked about her daughter or been in touch with us at all for nearly two years.

"Hey, Gus." My heart sinks. Darien's voice is exactly as I remember it. Low. Gravelly. Too fucking intense. My legs shiver as she settles herself on the porch swing, letting Winter slip to the dusty floorboards. I force my feet to carry me up the steps, where I sit, too.

Not all the way at the top, but close enough. My instinct is to grab my niece. Pull her to me. But my sister is nothing if not a paradox. Daring to want what she gave up will only draw her closer.

Instead I force myself to look at *her*. Darien radiates danger in a way Danny didn't. Her shoulder-length hair's been bleached, dyed, faded. I catch a hint of pink, green, but it's mostly a brassy blond. She's taken her piercings out and isn't wearing any makeup, and the result is that she's more startling than ever. It's her eyes. They're big and blue and also sunken so deep into her skull that they imply wisdom. Or knowledge. At twenty-eight, my sister has neither.

"You clean?" I ask.

"What does it look like?"

"You don't want me to answer that."

She laughs, a rich baritone roll that reminds me why people can love her. Why I loved her. Darien's the perfect blend of cynicism and indulgence, a bitter alchemy that can command attention from the most unlikely sources. I know this because I used to look up to her. She was everything to me, once, and I ache to have her near. I ache for her to love herself.

"You look like you want something," I say.

My sister rolls her eyes. "I hear you're the hotshot swimmer now. Danny's gone and now you're the one using all your daddy's money trying to make it in the record books. It's not worth it, if you ask me. You should be able to live your life without needing everyone to watch you do it."

"You should leave."

"I'm playing with my daughter. You got a problem with that?"

"Where's Mom?"

"Inside."

"I should get her."

"No, don't!" Darien rises from the swing and comes to me. She slides her way down the stairs and wraps an arm around my shoulder. "I'm sorry. It's just . . . she said we could have a few minutes. Just Winnie and I."

"And then what?"

"Then I'll be out of your life again. Don't worry, kid. I'm not here to fuck up your life. Or hers. Not any more than I already have."

I feel sick. "How much did she give you?"

Darien shrugs. "Enough."

"Enough that you'll sign those papers? That you'll let her have Winter?"

"Why do you care? You hate Mom. I know you do. You always have."

"Well, I guess I hate you, too," I say.

Her lips purse. "You know, you sound like Danny."

"Danny's dead."

Darien falters, a flash of pain crossing her face, lowering her voice. "I know. Mom called me when it happened."

My chest tightens. "You knew? Why didn't you come? I needed you."

"I couldn't do it," she says. Then: "I'm sorry, Gus. That was shitty. It was selfish."

I don't answer.

"You doing okay?" she asks.

My words are hard to get out. Like razor wire pulled across scarred skin. "I guess."

"You're the best of us, kid. You always have been. You have to know that."

"That's not saying a lot."

Darien laughs and reaches to touch my hair, to tousle it like she used to, and I don't really want her to but I let her do it because I guess I want someone to want to touch me, which is confusing, even to me. But as her fingers make contact, as they weave their way through my hair, I bend toward her, a bloom seeking light in the darkness.

"How're things going with her?" Darien asks. "I know it can't be easy. She's all denial about Danny."

"How so?"

"She keeps saying she doesn't know why he did it. Why he would hurt her like that. But, like, even I could see it coming."

"You did?"

"You didn't?"

"I don't know. I don't think I knew Danny very well. He mostly made me angry."

"Pretty sure that's how he made everyone feel."

"What does that mean?"

"Just that it's probably a shitty thing to go through life with everyone being mad at you all the time."

"Yeah." The sadness returns, fluttering down to darken my sky. "I guess I always thought he liked it. Like he thrived on people being mad at him. Hating him for what he could do."

"Maybe. I always got the feeling Danny got angry at himself as much as he made other people feel that way. It was like he didn't know any other way of being who he was."

"So who was he?" I ask.

"Hell if I know." Darien sits up, scratches her neck, then slides her phone out. She reads something off the screen. "I should get going."

"Okay."

"I'll see you around. Okay, kid?"

"Sure." I nod and smile, like that's something I'd like.

My sister gathers her purse, kisses Winter on the forehead, and turns around. She walks quickly down the steps and heads for the gate, then the street, and then she's gone and she doesn't look back. Not at me. Or the house. Or her daughter.

107.

"Let's go for a drive," I tell my mom on the day that marks one year since Danny died. Sitting around the house and moping all day feels unfathomable and thinking about her doing the same is even worse.

"Sure," she says. "But after the cemetery."

"Whatever." The cemetery isn't a place I'd planned to visit. This is for a lot of reasons, but mostly because I don't believe there's any piece of my brother buried there. He's gone. He's only a memory now. But having a place to go clearly means something to my mother. So we do.

The cemetery's tucked into a slice of Lafayette hillside, and it's surrounded by trees and foliage. Hummingbirds abound, buzzing and diving, and from a watchful distance, I hold Winter in my arms while my mom arranges flowers by Danny's headstone. When she reaches to touch the etched letters of his name, I turn away. I don't want to see this. Her tenderness that's always been reserved for him and only him.

I can't.

Once we're on the road again, I just want to keep going. We head south, navigating through winding mountains and towering redwoods before dipping down toward the ocean. Soon we reach Santa Cruz, a city disguised as a beach town or a beach town disguised as a city. We walk out on the pier and listen to the plaintive barks of the elephant seals before finding a restaurant that looks kid-friendly enough to handle Winter. She's extra pleased about the choice when she's handed a place mat decorated in sea animals, along with a box of crayons.

"I like it here," my mom says once she's settled in the booth. Once she can see the view. All those frothy ocean waves.

"Me too."

Her fingers work to unknot her napkin. "I wish you'd helped me with the flowers today. Or any day."

I look at her.

"Well, I do," she says.

"I can't," I tell her. "Not yet."

Her lips purse. "You're still mad about—"

"A lot of things."

My mother nods and looks out the window at the ocean. The waves are roiling, topped with white and crashing every which way. "You don't want to talk about him, do you?"

"Not really."

"Then tell me about something else."

So I do. I tell her about my own swimming and not only what I hope to do in Omaha, but how it makes me feel to be in the water. How I feel closer to my father there, skimming above the lane lines with shadows spinning all around me, and how maybe the imagery is too womblike, but that I don't care. It's my truth and it means something to me. It means a lot, actually.

She smiles a little when I say this, her gaze growing distant at the mention of my father.

"You hate me, don't you?" I blurt out. "For him dying the way he did. Because of me."

My mother starts back to the present. "Oh, come on. You know I don't hate you."

"No, I don't know that. How could I? You've always loved Danny more. You said I couldn't need you, because he needed you more."

"I never said that."

"You did!"

She shakes her head. "Well, I don't remember that. But Danny had a lot of problems when he was young. He did need me."

"You know what I think?" I tell her. "I think you're the one who needed him. And he knew that. When he was sick and upset as a kid—he used that to keep you close to him. He manipulated you."

Her eyes flash. "He was a *child*."

"Well, that's what it seemed like to me. And I was a child, too. But you and him had some sort of bond that I wasn't allowed to be a part of. Ever. And I don't even blame him for wanting to keep you close, but it sucked for me."

"So you're blaming me? For what? Your lack of happiness? Or his?"

"I'm not blaming anyone. I'm telling you how I feel."

My mother falls back against the booth seat and throws her hands up. "What do you want me to say? After your father died, yes, I needed Danny. I needed *someone*. I hated my life and a lot of times I hated the person that I was."

"I'm sorry," I say.

"Do you know how hard it was to be on my own with three kids? Do you know how hard it still is?"

I line Winter's crayons up in front of her, tuck a curl behind her ear. "No."

"But . . ." My mother softens. "I don't hate you, Gus. I promise. And I don't blame you for what happened to your father. Not at all. Why would you think that?"

"It's what Darien told me."

"Really?"

"Yes. Really. Danny, too. He was there when she said it."

She rolls her eyes. Dips a french fry in ketchup before placing it in her mouth. "God, they were both such assholes, sometimes."

"Yeah."

"I guess I just hate that he died at all," she says with a sigh.

I lower my head in response, focus on my food. I mean, I'm not sure who the *he* is in this statement. My father? Danny? But I don't bother asking or pushing for more. Another time, maybe.

For now, it's enough.

~~~~~~~~~~~

Later we walk down the boardwalk, stepping into the sand. Winter's wild in the presence of so much stimulation. The rides. The lights. The food. My mother runs ahead with her, offering promises of a carousel ride or the Ferris wheel, if only she'll slow down.

For my part, I'm a mess—jumpy, irritable, and torn between my usual urges of throwing myself into the waves or needing god-like power in order to control the tides and everything else in my universe. But it's okay to feel this way. That's what I decide. My brother's been dead for a year, my father far longer, and I remain endlessly angry and bitter about both these truths. But maybe this is just what grief is.

Maybe this is what my mother was trying to tell me.

108.

I should probably ask Coach Marks before I do what I'm about to do. But then I probably wouldn't do it in the first place. Besides, I'm impulsive. So what I do is this: I rummage around in my room until I find Renee Matheson's business card. She's the reporter from *Swimming World* who I met with in San Diego last September.

With what I hope are only good intentions, I call her. I end up leaving a message, but she calls back the next day and we talk for a long time. About everything that matters to me.

Danny.

Depression.

Suicide.

Survivorship.

Anger.

Trauma.

Guilt.

Grief.

Self-harm.

Self-loathing.

All of it.

I also tell her about black swan theory and how trying to understand the past is just a way of trying to understand yourself so that you can figure out a way to move forward in an uncertain world. That within all of us lies the ability to grow and learn and adapt and get better at what it is we want to achieve. We just have to be here in order to do that.

Danny didn't get that chance, I tell her. He's not here, and for all our conflict and toxic sibling resentment, I wish like hell he were. It took me a while to realize this. For so long, I was the floundering goose to his swanlike glory that it was difficult for me to accept his pain as anything other than a tool meant to punish me. Plus, my mind was working so hard to define his death as something inevitable, I almost didn't see my own coming. But then I got lucky. I had people around me who cared enough to make sure I got help when I needed it.

Who couldn't bear another fallen bird in their midst.

I tell her everything. About hurting myself and the people around me. About therapy and meds and how they've helped and yet I'm still me—endlessly flawed and lit by fire. Sometimes this fire is the same one that fuels me in the pool, in practice, but it can't be the whole of my being. Not without burning me alive. And I also tell her how I really don't have any answers. I'm still unsure about so much. But the one thing I know is that sometimes you need other people and that there's no weakness in that. None.

"So are you doing this for him?" Renee Matheson asks, because this is what everyone always asks of me. "The Trials, I mean."

"Yes," I say. "I'm doing this for him. I just wish I didn't have to."

109.

There's no send-off party for me before the Trials. No fanfare or fuss. Coach M and I fly out to Omaha on Thursday morning—my mother will come tomorrow—and while I'm on the flight, I tell myself the lack of attention is a blessing. It's all on account of my weak qualifying performance. I'm not expected to do anything—I'm just supposed to feel lucky for the opportunity. But that's a game I already know can be won.

I've seen it happen, after all.

We land and sit on the tarmac. I turn my phone on while we wait for a gate and when I do, there're tons of messages. It's more than a little baffling, since it's not like I have a ton of friends. But the first is from Lynette:

Good luck, Gus! she writes. *We're so proud of you.*

I smile. It turns out there's one from Caleb, too.

Good luck, man. You got this.

Then I see ones from Vince and Raheem and the rest of the team. I keep scrolling because even my cold cynical heart is warmed by their well-wishes. Fitz's makes me smile:

On the day we met I told you how much I admired your brother. Now I can add you to the list of assholes I look up to.

I read Lainey's last.

I'll be watching, she tells me. *Remember that it's okay to feel scared! Or not! However you feel is just right.*

110

We tour the aquatic facility Friday night before the Trials. It's an indoor pool and Coach Marks walks me through my race, the schedule, all the quirks of the event. I won't actually be in the water until Sunday, and it's eerie how quiet the space is. We sit for a moment in the upper deck and I breathe it in. This moment.

This possibility.

"Nervous?" he asks.

"Definitely. What about you?"

"Closer to terrified."

"Sounds about right," I say, and I wait a beat before asking my next question. It's one I've been thinking about a lot. "Why do you think he did it?"

Coach M turns to me. "Danny?"

"Yeah."

He shakes his head. "God, I don't know."

"You spent so much time with him."

"I did. But I don't have any answers. I've second-guessed myself a lot about the way I trained him, the way I treated him. But I had no idea. Not until . . . closer to the end. By the time I realized he was sick, I did what I could to get him help, but it didn't make him very happy with me."

I sit up. "What did you do?"

"I told his coach at UCLA about his history with anxiety and insomnia. Said that he needed to stay in treatment and stay on his meds while he was competing."

"Did he?"

"I don't know. He was an adult, by then. No one could make him do anything. But Lyle asked me for my honest assessment of what would make Danny successful, and Danny took it as a betrayal. Wouldn't talk to me after that. I never heard from him again."

I'm stunned. "That's really shitty. I didn't know that."

"Yeah."

"Wait, did you get the letter he wrote you? I left it in your house. On Thanksgiving." My cheeks warm at the mention of that ill-fated holiday. "It was for you, right? It was your address. I found it in his car."

"It was for me. And I did get it. Thank you."

"Did he forgive you?"

The smile Coach Marks offers me is a sad one. "He was pretty unwell when he wrote it. Still angry. I think he was mostly saying good-bye."

"Fuck," I say.

He dips his head. "Did you know that Renee sent me a copy of your interview?"

My pulse quickens. "She did?"

"It's going to run tomorrow, just in time for the Trials."

"Win or lose," I say. "I guess it'll all be out there."

Coach M lifts an eyebrow. "I didn't know you thought about losing."

"I mean, I kind of have to, don't I? I've figured that much out by now. With your help. And my therapist's. So yeah, I have a plan for dealing with whatever the hell happens on Sunday. Win or lose, I'll be okay."

"Glad to hear it."

I smile. "I'm still going to win, though."

"I know you will." He claps my back. "And by the way, that interview, I really enjoyed it."

"You did?"

"That took a lot of courage. More than I have, that's for sure.

It's going to do a lot of good for a lot of people, okay? People who need to hear what you have to say."

I bite my lip. Every part of me wants to thank him or tell him he's the reason I have any courage at all, but it's hard right now and I can't and that's stupid. But he knows, I think. He wraps his arms around me and holds me to him.

"Oh, Gus," he says. "This is going to hurt for a long time. Forever, maybe. It's damn sad what happened. There's no way around that. But I'm glad you're here. And I'm glad I've gotten to know you."

111.

On Sunday morning, I walk onto the pool deck with a myriad of emotions, thoughts, swirling through my veins. It's my first heat of the day and the crowd is huge—nearly ten thousand people, every one of them waving tiny red, white, and blue flags—and the sheer mass of their presence is enough to generate its own force. Its own energy.

My insignificance feels staggering. I do what I can to hold my own in the presence of so many legends, so much history, and I know I'm not here by myself. Somewhere in that vibrant, raucous crowd, my mother is watching me, along with Winter. Coach M is out there, too, of course. Plus there's Vince and Fitz and everyone back home. Even Lainey, I remind myself, who I have to hope knows how much I care for her and how much I appreciate the kindness she showed me at a time when I didn't understand that kindness was even something to be valued.

Danny and my father aren't far from my thoughts, either. They never are, and there's nothing comfortable that comes from thinking about them. But what I've learned over this past year is that every life contains tragedy. Every story is born from loss. And no, I don't know how to reconcile the different parts of me and my story—the anger and resentment, the guilt and the shame—but I know I'll always be connected to my family in ways both good and bad. In ways I have yet to figure out.

But for now, how can I be anything but grateful?

Maybe a little heartbroken, too.

My chest tightens as my name's called over the loudspeaker and I walk to my lane on trembling legs. To tamp down my nerves, I focus on the little things. I adjust my goggles. I take deep breaths. This is it.

The ref whistles, signaling swimmers up, and I step onto the block. Only I don't stare down at the water, at what lies below. Instead I lift my head and gaze out at the thousands of eager faces all staring back at me. For the briefest of moments, just a quick heartbeat of life, I inhale their passion, their thrill, their sound and their fury—all that they're willing to give.

This is what I'll carry with me.

This is what will bring me home.

"Take your mark," the ref calls, and it's time. I bend into my starting stance and work to steady myself, ensuring that every muscle is coiled and ready. A hush falls over the crowd—that cover of pure stillness or as close to it as I've ever heard—and *this* is what true anticipation looks like. The conviction that all that comes next will matter.

You want to know what I really and truly love about this moment?

Whether goose or swan, I have wings.

And I'll fly.

Below is a list of organizations and resources available to support the mental well-being of student athletes:

The Hidden Opponent

Raising awareness for student-athlete mental health, the Hidden Opponent empowers athletes to face the hidden opponent together as a community.

instagram.com/thehiddenopponent/

Michael Phelps Foundation

Focused on promoting water safety, healthy living (mental and physical), and the pursuit of dreams, especially for children.

michaelphelpsfoundation.org

The original art presented in this book was curated by TaskForce, a creative agency that collaborates with the most influential non-profits, brands, and people taking on the most pressing challenges facing our state, our nation, and our world. TaskForce builds capacity and community for those shaping a more empathetic society through public opinion and policy.

For more information, please visit taskforce.pr.

Artist Biographies

Artists are listed in the order in which their work appears in the book.

Bedelgeuse (Travis Bedel)
Bedelgeuse is the anatomical collage work and alias for artist Travis Bedel. Travis's wild amalgamation of botanical, zoological, and anatomical imagery produces synergistic visuals that represent humanity's inherent relationship to nature and the universe.

I sought to manifest an image that represented the crushing darkness of depression. Predatory sea creatures and kelp wrap around the figure, as if to keep them drowned in the grips of their suffering. From above, they are being pulled toward sparkling light from the surface, out from the darkness below.

Deedee Cheriel
Deedee Cheriel is an Indian American artist living and working in Los Angeles. With influences derived from such opposites as East Indian temple imagery, punk rock, and her Pacific Northwest natural environment, her images are indications of how we try to connect ourselves to others and how these satirical and heroic efforts are episodes of compassion and discomfort.

In searching for an image to create for this book, I wanted to use bold loose strokes to convey flow and movement. I used white to create negative spaces to convey beauty and tension, overlapping them with bold images of anthropomorphic beings connecting and disconnecting with others.

Adam Enrique Rodriguez

Born and raised in Indio, California, Adam Enrique Rodriguez is known for his signature style of deconstructed faces and human figures. He incorporates abstraction with classical aspects, in an ongoing conversation around psychology and the human condition.

Rodriguez has made art for charitable and community organizations, as well as more than twenty large-scale murals in commercial spaces, private residences, and music festivals throughout California.

For my work in Geese Are Never Swans, *I highlight the intensity of the story's vibrant character; the passion and the confusion in the life of a young athlete navigating through personal traumas, mental health, and triumphs; and the raw emotion of the human experience that connects us all.*

Augustine Kofie

Born and based in Los Angeles and active in the Southern California graffiti scene since the midnineties, Augustine Kofie works in painting, collage, and mural interventions. Kofie's fine art practice draws together the languages of graffiti's deconstructive lettering, street culture, mechanical drafting, modern architecture, contemporary music, and 1960s–80s iconography.

My painting is inspired by the novel's aquatic theme in its palette of blues, greens, and aquamarines, as well as its compositional elements of ripple and reflection. Like much of my work, the painting harmonizes opposing and contradictory dynamics in a quest for balance. In this, it reflects Gus's quest to find a path through the struggles and challenges of his life. Sport, like art, becomes a way to organize one's feelings, to take control of the breakage, and to create order out of chaos.

Najeebah Al-Ghadban (front cover collage)

Najeebah Al-Ghadban is a designer and collage artist from Kuwait. Her collage work has been featured in the *New York Times Magazine*, the *California Sunday Magazine*, and *Anxy* magazine. She is currently a designer for the NYT Mag Labs in New York.

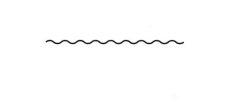

KOBE BRYANT was an Academy Award winner, a *New York Times* best-selling author, and the CEO of Granity Studios, a multimedia content creation company. He was also a five-time NBA champion, two-time NBA Finals MVP, NBA MVP, and two-time Olympic gold medalist. In everything he built, Kobe was driven to teach the next generation how to reach their full potential. He believed in the beauty of the process, in the strength that comes from inner magic, and in achieving the impossible. His legacy continues today.

~~~~~~~~~~

EVA CLARK is a psychologist and an award-winning young adult novelist. As a psychologist, she focuses on mental health, social justice, and sports. As an author, her focus is on creating stories that help young people discover their best selves. She lives in California with her family.

GRANITY STUDIOS, LLC

GRANITYSTUDIOS.COM

Library of Congress Control Number: 2019954481
ISBN (hardcover): 9781949520057
ISBN (eBook): 9781949520064

Printed in the United States of America
1 3 5 7 9 10 8 6 4 2

Book design by Karina Granda
Type design by November
Art direction by Sharanya Durvasula

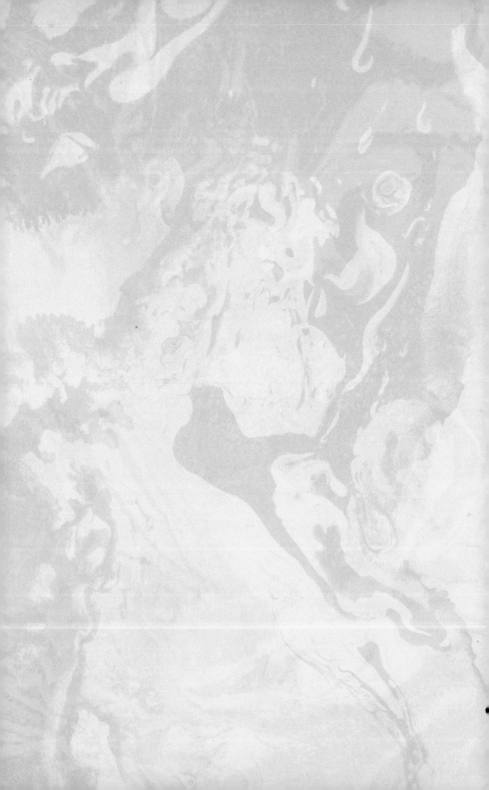